Pr
an

MW01258272

"The Uplift books are as compulsive reading as
anything ever published in the genre."
—*The Encyclopedia of Science Fiction*

THE UPLIFT WAR

"An exhilarating read that encompasses everything from breathless
action to finely drawn moments of quiet intimacy. There is no way
we can avoid coming back as many times as Brin wants us to do,
until his story is done."
—*Locus*

"Shares all the properties that made *Startide Rising* such a joy. The plot
fizzes along . . . and there are the wonders of the Galactic civilizations
(which have all the invention and excitement that SF *used* to have)."
—*Asimov's Science Fiction*

SUNDIVER

"Brin has done a superb job on all counts."
—*Science Fiction Times*

"Brin has a fertile and well-developed imagination . . .
coupled with a sinuous and rapid-paced style."
—*Heavy Metal*

STARTIDE RISING

"An extraordinary achievement, a book so full of fascinating ideas
that they would not have crowded each other at
twice its considerable length."
—Poul Anderson

"One of the outstanding SF novels of recent years."
—*Publishers Weekly*

BRIGHTNESS REEF

"Boils with plots and subplots."
—*San Francisco Sunday Examiner & Chronicle*

"Brin is a skillful storyteller....
There is more than enough action to keep the book exciting,
and like all good serials, the first volume ends with a bang."
—*The Plain Dealer*

"A captivating read...*Brightness Reef* leaves you looking forward
to more. It's a worthy addition to what promises to be
a great science-fiction series."
—*Star Tribune,* Minneapolis

"Brin has shown beyond a doubt that he is a master of plot and
character and incident, of sheer storytelling, while he is also
thoughtful enough to satisfy anyone's craving for meat on those
literary bones. Don't miss this one, folks, or the next."
—*Analog*

INFINITY'S SHORE

"Well paced, immensely complex, highly literate...On full display here
is Brin's extraordinary capacity to handle a wide-ranging narrative
and to create convincingly complex alien races....Superior SF."
—*Publishers Weekly*

"Here, again, David Brin displays the considerable expertise in
universe-building which has garnered him numerous awards. And,
again, he proves himself to be a very gifted storyteller."
—*Mysterious Galaxy*

HEAVEN'S REACH

"Brin, as usual, provides loads of action as he presents a
galactic panorama to view and intellectual speculation
to challenge the reader."
—*Sunday Life*

CONTACTING
ALIENS

David Brin's UPLIFT series:

CONTACTING ALIENS

An Illustrated Guide to David Brin's Uplift Universe

David Brin
and Kevin Lenagh

BANTAM BOOKS

CONTACTING ALIENS

PUBLISHING HISTORY
A Bantam Spectra trade paperback / July 2002
SPECTRA and the portrayal of a boxed "s" are trademarks of Bantam Books,
a division of Random House, Inc.

LIBRARY OF CONGRESS CATALOGING-IN-PUBLICATION DATA

Brin, David.
Contacting aliens : an illustrated guide to David Brin's uplift universe /
David Brin and Kevin Lenagh.
p. cm.
Includes index.
ISBN 0-553-37796-5
1. Brin, David—Handbooks, manuals, etc. 2. Science fiction, American—
Handbooks, manuals, etc. I. Lenagh, Kevin. II. Title.

PS3552.R4825 Z464 2002
813'.54—dc21
2001056643

Published simultaneously in the United States and Canada

Bantam Books are published by Bantam Books, a division of Random House,
Inc. Its trademark, consisting of the words "Bantam Books" and the portrayal of
a rooster, is Registered in U.S. Patent and Trademark Office and in other
countries. Marca Registrada. Bantam Books, 1540 Broadway, New York,
New York 10036.

PRINTED IN THE UNITED STATES OF AMERICA

RRH   10 9 8 7 6 5 4 3 2 1

For Sandra, my rock, who made it happen.

—Kevin Lenagh

To those earlier "alien designers"... Barlowe and Clements, Burns and Vinge, Cherryh and Niven... living proof that we can build 'em. So let them come.

—David Brin

Contents

foreword

Welcome to the Adventure

Congratulations. If you are reading this, you are among those chosen—
after rigorous screening—to share confidential data about aliens.

This handbook was created to assist in the training of Terragen
Field Agents. As a top-secret, eyes-only survey, it is designed to help
you, the student, understand many of the dangers and perplexing situations you will face during missions representing the three sapient
races of Earth throughout the vast and dangerous Civilization of Five
Galaxies.

We begin this volume by briefly reviewing Earth's difficult history
since first contact with Galactic culture, including recent events that
brought us to a critical point in our relationship with that ancient, mysterious, and powerful civilization. Then we will survey a wide range of
alien species, clans, and alliances, concentrating on those offering the
greatest threat or hope to Earthclan during our time of crisis.

> This information is for use by agents and
> trainees of the Terragen Field Service. Unautho-
> rized possession of this document carries a
> penalty of lifetime supervised probation and/or
> exile under the Earthclan Security Act.

You may be wondering why this report exists only on old-fashioned paper pages featuring flat, immobile illustrations, holding just enough data for a cursory summary. More extensive reports can be found in branch units of the Great Galactic Library, but recall that nearly all Library entries were written by nonhumans. Automated translation lets us read them in Anglic, Rossic, Nihanic, Han, French, and other Earthly tongues, but how much is lost in the process? Even in a Galactic language, there remain questions of editorial bias. So it was decided to offer trainees this supplemental collection of impressions gathered by experienced human operatives, outside the influence of any Galactic Institution.

Why paper pages? Non-Earthlings are so used to accessing information from muon-nudged Library data blips that most would not recognize the old-style book you are holding as a form of data representation! Even those non-Terrans who grasp the concept will be disdainful of our primitive "wolfling" technology.

Nevertheless, you students must remember your oaths and treat this book as a relic-secret of vital importance to our world, our clan, and the Three Sapient Species of Earth.

This Guide and How It Works

This guide is organized to help the field agent quickly reference friend or foe. Clans are organized in chronological order of Uplift; however, actual power and control of the clan may not be in the "hands" of the oldest species. The most influential races in each clan are listed in **bold.**

part 1:

THE GALAXIES

History

Almost three centuries after human-alien contact, we are now used to seeing members of some Galactic sapient race strolling the streets of an Earth city, often accompanied by a duenna-robot for "protection on a primitive world."

Only in Reserve Areas can humans, neo-Chimps, and neo-Dolphins escape frequent reminders that the universe has arrived and is here to stay. Basic Galactography and Sapientology are taught in schools. It takes a stretch of imagination to recall what it was like so long ago, when we thought ourselves alone in the cosmos.

Duenna bots

Back in the early 22nd century, many decades before contact, the Solar Confederation approved construction of several antimatter-driven starships for the purpose of exploring nearby star systems. Early vessels of the unmanned Hawking class plunged beyond the orbit of Pluto, then the cometary Oort Cloud in the late 2100s. Later, the first human-crewed vessels—*Isaac Newton* and *Jane Chen*—departed, bound for the Tau Ceti and Alpha Centauri systems. Even allowing for relativistic effects, these missions involved long periods of hibernation for the crew, who never expected to see home again.

Leaders of Earth had prepared contingency plans for encountering other life-forms, but the first seven expeditions found only ruined worlds in the Geminga Starfield, the local zone surrounding our solar system. Soon, this region came to be known as *The Ash*, for its disheartening array of burned-out planetary ecosystems. Civilization *had*

Hawking class unmanned probe

once swarmed across this sector, it seemed, but those former occupants left behind only deserts and desolation. Now our part of the universe was empty and humankind seemed to be alone.

Who could tell how far The Ash extended? For all we knew, it might stretch to the limits of the Galaxy. Perhaps this was the reason we had been alone for so long?

Thus it came as a shock when the Earth ship *Vesarius* had a sudden chance meeting with the Tymbrimi vessel *Cuthmar.* No one had envisioned encountering a civilization as vast and complex as that of the Galactics—so incredibly ancient, so fearsomely intricate and dangerous, spanning not one but *five* galaxies! Beyond the narrow moat of The Ash, there dwelled a bewildering range of beings whose powers seemed nearly godlike.

Our predicament was made worse by the fact that Terrans were the first "wolfling" clan discovered in several million years.

As the most primitive starfaring race seen in eons, we had reason for worry! How well we recalled the fate of indigenous peoples back in the 16th and 17th centuries, who suffered when they were overwhelmed by European technology. The disaster at NuDawn only reinforced our fears about what seemed to lie in store for Terran civilization.

Two lucky strokes saved us from immediate and dire consequences.

Our first break came at the very moment of contact, because we ran into the Tymbrimi before any other race. Though often quirky or irksome, the Tymbrimi have proved helpful friends. Their advice proved crucial on many occasions.

The other piece of good fortune had roots in the very nature of Galactic culture. Vastly older than we could have imagined, the loose Civilization of Five Galaxies is founded on a single unifying principle, that of *Uplift.* Under this ancient tradition, older species continually "adopt" younger, promising races that have not yet reached full sapiency, raising them up to starfaring status. Ideally, each client race then earns the right to uplift clients of its own, continuing a line of succession that is much like raising children—when it works well—a cycle of sponsorship stretching back to the misty dawn of Galactic civilization, the era of the fabled *Progenitors*.

By fortunate happenstance, humanity had already engaged in this "sacred" activity, not once but twice, just before contact! After two centuries of genetic and cultural experimentation, the Solar Confederation had just granted citizenship rights to neo-Chimpanzees (*Pan sapiens*), and was about to give neo-Dolphins (*Tursiops amicus*) similar status. Thus we were already "patrons" to two client races.

Because of this remarkable coincidence—and by using some fancy political maneuvering—our Tymbrimi friends lobbied for us and won formal recognition of humanity's patron status, with all the rights and responsibilities that attain thereto. This astonishing coup was unprecedented. On occasion, other "wolfling" races had been discovered, but never before was one elevated suddenly to the middle ranks of Galactic Society.

This victory turned out to be a mixed blessing, provoking friction with some of the more conservative factions in ET culture. Several hostile groups keep trying to prove that humans are unfit to be patrons. They aim to have humankind—as well as Dolphins and Chimps—put up for adoption. "To a trustworthy guide," as a Soro breed-mother once put it, "for the Earthlings' own good."

CUTHMAR meeting VESARIUS

We must assuage these groups, not giving them any cause for griev-
ance. For this reason, the Terragen Uplift Oversight Committee and
Foundation for Promotion of Sapience abide strictly by Galactic rules in
continuing work on neo-Dolphins and neo-Chimps.

In brief, we must be a very clever little tribe, using diplomacy, flattery, and sometimes trickery, striving to win friends and keep mighty
forces at bay as we study hard to catch up.

History warns of dire penalties if we fail.

"Ever since humans dreamed of landing on the moon, we
also imagined making contact with other civilizations. Most
of those fantasies, during that long period of isolation, pic-
tured us being strong, adventurous, expansive—all ideals left
over from the Euro-Western 'frontier.' Now we find that humans are the primitive, helpless ones, at the mercy of a titanic
civilization we can barely fathom. Earthlings must adjust to
that fact, or risk the same fate as our ancestors who were Native Americans, Africans, and islanders. We must adapt, study,
and above all else, *buy time!*

"It's that or die."

—*Jacob Demwa, First Advisor,*
Terragen Uplift Foundation

Timeline

NOTE: This is based on historical summaries offered by Earth's branch unit of the Galactic Library. For some reason this unit grows ambiguous and evasive as we look further back in time, using language that becomes increasingly vague and oracular. Entries over 300 million years old must be taken as only generally valid, and possibly mythological.

3.1 BILLION–2.8 BILLION YEARS AGO ▶ Massive terraforming campaigns separately transform Galaxies One and Two. Evidence of repeated world-shattering conflicts leaving vast domains of "ash." Few decipherable records remain, though evidence points to an age of domination by the Machine Order.

2.8 BILLION–2.2 BILLION YEARS AGO ▶ Oxygen-breathing cultures in Galaxy One discover whorl-link to Galaxy Two. A combined civilization emerges, then dissolves in horrible war. Only the Progenitors survive. The Paean of Loneliness appears to date from this age, as they search among the animals for potential companions and begin the process of Uplift. (At this time, early single-cell organisms dwell in Earth's seas.)

2.71 BILLION YEARS AGO ▶ Transfer point to Galaxy Three discovered; traces of wrecked Galactic-level civilization discovered there.

2.7 BILLION YEARS AGO ▶ First Machine Wars. Resurgent AIs nearly recover their former dominance. Digital cognizance and nanotechnology restricted. Institute for Foresight is created.

2.3 BILLION YEARS AGO ▶ Progenitors retire, gradually separating themselves from affairs of lesser races, leaving behind laws and edicts regarding tradition of Uplift.

2.26 BILLION YEARS AGO ▶ Progenitors physically leave the "Many Galaxies" (according to Inheritor legend), or transcend (by Awaitor lore) to another plane of reality.

2.25 BILLION YEARS AGO ▶ Contact made with Galaxies Four through Eleven. War breaks out with hydrogen-breather civilization spreading from Galaxy Six. Both cultures are nearly ruined before coexistence is established via treaty with the Zang. Few reliable details about this agreement are accessible to sapients in our life-order and at our status level.

2.22 BILLION YEARS AGO ▶ Progenitors "pass on" (according to the Transcendor faith).

2.2 BILLION YEARS AGO ▶ After a near-total collapse, Galactic society attempts to reorganize without Progenitors, aided by an early version of the Great Library.

2.1(?) BILLION–1.9 BILLION YEARS AGO ▶ Formative stages of present Galactic civilization.

1.9 BILLION YEARS AGO ▶ Institute for Civilized Warfare formed.

1.6 BILLION YEARS AGO ▶ Contact is lost with galaxies that had (till then) been designated numbers Seven, Nine, and Eleven. Remaining galaxies are renumbered One through Eight. Cultural upheavals. First wave of memnetic plagues.

1.4 BILLION YEARS AGO ▶ Modern Library and Uplift Institutes reorganized and essentially assume their modern forms. (Eukaryotic organisms take sway in Earth's seas. Primitive life-forms colonize land.)

1.1 BILLION YEARS AGO ▶ Contact lost with Galaxy Eight. Memnetic plagues lead to lawless warfare and spread of Ash.

830 MILLION YEARS AGO ▶ Contact temporarily lost with Galaxy Five. (Earth begins to explode with multicellular sea life.)

620 MILLION YEARS AGO ▶ The "Lions" seize control of many spiral arms, flouting tradition, colonizing, and terraforming without restriction. Ash spreads through 30 percent of Galaxy One and 20 percent of Galaxy Two. (Complex organisms swarm Earth seas.)

618 MILLION YEARS AGO ▶ The Tarseuh forge a coalition to overthrow the "Lions." Communications are seriously disrupted. Contact with Galaxies Two and Six permanently lost. Galaxies renumbered again.

598 MILLION YEARS AGO ▶ Ultraconservative Institute for Recovery of Honor, dedicated to repairing damage wrought by the "Lions," dominates main Galaxies. It has since become dormant.

590 MILLION YEARS AGO ▶ Institute for Recovery of Honor wracked by ideological disputes; Obeyor/Abdicator holy war results. This is judged to have been a memnetic "plague" outbreak as moderate consensus emerges from chaos.

400 MILLION YEARS AGO ▶ An abused client race, the Karrank%, are released from clienthood and granted the planet Kithrup as a "recuperation home."

320 MILLION YEARS AGO ▶ Contact temporarily lost with Galaxy Three, where Hydrogen and Oxygen civilizations engage in high levels of cooperation. Flat-space expeditions sent toward lost galaxies to discover their fate. (Era of amphibians on Earth.)

280 MILLION YEARS AGO ▶ "Revolt of the Data." Subtle memnetic diseases affect nearly all computers. Outbreak, blamed on Machine Order, is suppressed violently. Library purged of seditious or "irrelevant" information. Present system of neutral/passive data storage instituted, promised to be plague-resistant.

230 MILLION YEARS AGO ▶ First "Gronin Collapse" of Galactic society. Library purges reach a point where major blocks of information are deeply sequestered and possibly lost.

205 MILLION YEARS AGO ▶ A time of intense rebuilding. The Institute of Progress is raised to the highest point in its history as research and learning become important again for a while. (Age of the dinosaurs on Earth.)

150 MILLION YEARS AGO ▶ Social discord over redevelopment initiates a second "Gronin Collapse." Loss of contact with Galaxies Four and Seven. Remaining galaxies renumbered.

141 MILLION YEARS AGO ▶ All major sapient races form a union, slowly regaining confidence.

133 MILLION YEARS AGO ▶ Brief coalescence of oxygen- and hydrogen-breathing cultures in Galaxy Three ends when that galaxy is re-united with the others.

60 MILLION YEARS AGO ▶ A medium-scale "Time of Crisis." A zone of ash forms in Earth-local space. Twelve-Spin machine civilization is scapegoated and suppressed. (Dinosaurs and many other life-forms die off on Earth, making way for Age of Mammals.)

41 MILLION YEARS AGO ▶ Rediscovery of transfer points to galaxies originally numbered Seven and Eleven, now renumbered Two and Four.

33 MILLION YEARS AGO ▶ Thennanin uplifted by the Wortl; join Abdicators Alliance.

12 MILLION YEARS AGO ▶ The last recorded "wolfling" race, the Paranaj, is discovered; within a few hundred years it is extinct. (Forebears of apes and humans dwell in African forests.)

2.1 MILLION YEARS AGO ▶ Soro uplifted by Hul. (*Homo erectus* starts to spread from Africa into Asia.)

50,000 YEARS AGO ▶ The Bururalli Holocaust wipes out most higher animals on planet Garth; the Bururalli are destroyed as punishment. The Nahalli ulsu-Bururalli are reduced to clienthood and indentured to the Thennanin for rehabilitation. (Humans on Earth showing early signs of agriculture, and control over domestic beasts.)

4,000 YEARS AGO ▶ Patrons of the Tymbrimi, the Caltmour, wiped out in Galactic war. The Institute for Civilized Warfare calls it an "unfortunate error." (Time of Egyptian Middle Kingdom on Earth.)

2,491 YEARS AGO ▶ Beginning of Common Era Calendar on Earth (1 A.D.).

531 YEARS AGO ▶ First human space travel.

431 YEARS AGO ▶ First human slower-than-light interstellar travel.

390–300 YEARS AGO ▶ Earth dominated by The Bureaucracy (2102–2192 C.E.).

389 YEARS AGO ▶ Effort begins to uplift Chimpanzees.

366 YEARS AGO ▶ Effort at Dolphin Uplift begins.

350 YEARS AGO ▶ NuDawn, our first interstellar human colony, settled on a promising world within The Ash.

290 YEARS AGO ▶ Jacob Demwa is born.

280 YEARS AGO ▶ First successful Galactic contact—by starship *Vesarius,* with Tymbrimi vessel *Cuthmar.* This was a little over 44 choduras ago, by Galactic measure.

279 YEARS AGO ▶ The Catastrophe at NuDawn. Earth's colony "sequestered" in a disastrous encounter with officials from the Migration Institute. Earth learns the news two years later.

265 YEARS AGO ▶ In a surprise diplomatic coup, humanity is formally recognized as a patron-class citizen race. Neo-Chimps and neo-Dolphins granted Stage 1 client status.

251 YEARS AGO ▶ Neo-Chimps recognized as Stage 2 clients.

249 YEARS AGO ▶ Small branch of the Great Galactic Library installed on Earth.

240 YEARS AGO ▶ *Sundiver* Incident (2246 A.D.). Humanity now has three colony worlds. In another surprising coup, Earth is granted mid-Planetary-sized Library branch as reparations for illegal activities by the Pila and Soro.

161 YEARS AGO ▶ Neo-Dolphins recognized as Stage 2 clients.

98 YEARS AGO ▶ Garth licensed to be colonized by the Terragens.

5 YEARS AGO ▶ Human-Galactic relations stable. There are now ten Terragen colonies, all of them except Calafia on less desirable "recovery worlds."

Dolphin-crewed STREAKER leaving spacedock

3 YEARS AGO ❱ Experimental Terragen survey ship *Streaker*—crewed by 120 Dolphins and 7 humans—encounters a fleet of ancient derelicts in an isolated Galactic tide pool; psi-cast message sends Galaxy One into turmoil. Corrupted Institutes prove incapable of intervening. *Streaker* forced to flee.

2 YEARS AGO ❱ Garth colony invaded by the Gubru. Invaders expelled after many months of struggle by the mixed Chimpanzee and human population.

2 YEARS AGO ▶ Intercepted Soro time-drop message reports that *Streaker* fled planet Kithrup in the Kthsemenee system. Images of the bizarre and wondrous incident on Garth transmitted throughout Galaxy via hyperspace shunt. Neo-Chimps achieve Stage 3, though their ceremony was interrupted. The Thennanin adopt neo-Gorillas as new clients and become reluctant Earth allies.

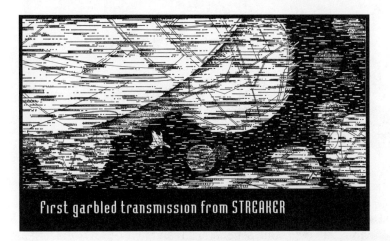

First garbled transmission from STREAKER

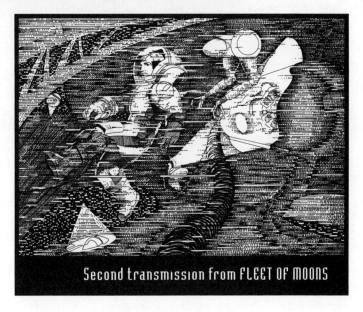

Second transmission from FLEET OF MOONS

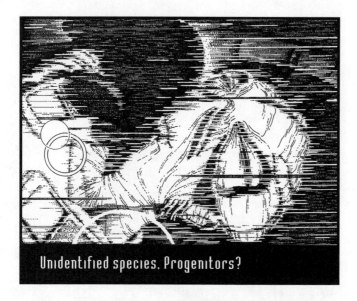

Unidentified species, Progenitors?

0–CURRENT DAY (2492 C.E.) ❯ Earth is temporarily safe thanks to our new Thennanin Alliance. But a general breakdown of law and order means that our colonies are in great peril. Also, rumors tell of plans by several major alliances to somehow coerce Earthclan into revealing secrets uncovered by *Streaker*. These plans may possibly include invasion by massive force.

50–1000 YEARS FROM NOW ❯ Horpie region to be opened for settlement sometime in this period, with Terragens holding three colony-option credits—assuming that law and Galactic Civilization still exist at that time. And that we still exist, too.

The Institutes

Governing Galactic Society

From trace records left by the first Galactic Golden Age, the earliest starfaring race—*the Progenitors*—realized that managing a cohesive centralized government was impossible between two planets, much less across several galaxies. But the alternative—letting diverse species engage in free-for-all battles over Galactic resources—would only result in more regions like The Ash, filling every spiral arm with desolation.

To prevent this, the Progenitors realized they must work *with* the drive for self-advancement that pulses within each race and individual. They came up with a plan to ensure that it is in everyone's self-interest to protect the future.

Status within the Five Galaxies is determined by how many new citizen species or "clients" your clan has uplifted. Nurturing newness is vital, so there must always be a supply of fresh, pre-sapient races to uplift. This means there is a premium on protecting Earth-like "nursery" worlds.

The resulting pan-Galactic society, with its strange eco-fanaticism, has posed many short-term unpleasant dilemmas to Earthclan. But the long-term logic makes sense. It prevents territories like The Ash from filling all of space. The success of fostering life for two billion years is hard to argue with. Things could have been worse.

Alas, the universe is still a hard place for "wolflings" like us.

While the oxygen-breathing Civilization of Five Galaxies lacks a central government, it does maintain influential agencies, or *Institutes*, which we'll now discuss.

The Institute for Uplift

 The Uplift Institute is among the most powerful, directly regulating the top ambition of each clan—to adopt new client species. Institute guidelines require that each new starfaring race meet several basic goals before graduation to full citizenship. Among other things, they must be able to pilot starships, engage in commerce and intellectual discourse, make long-range plans, regulate their own reproductive drives, and aspire to be patrons themselves, adding esteem to their clan and civilization as a whole. Institute inspectors are charged with protecting species undergoing Uplift, so the process is performed with fairness and compassion.

Unfortunately, these rules are often bent by strong clans such as the Tandu, who have bred their clients to a blind obedience. The N'8ght, Hul, and Nighthunters have also adjusted their clients for overdependence. (These scandals appear to have been squelched and full data is not available in open files of the Great Library.) Still, despite such bad examples, the Uplift Institute does much good. By dutifully reporting on progress with our neo-Dolphin and neo-Chimp clients, humanity has been able to enlist Institute aid, both in learning to be good patrons and keeping powerful clans from annexing Earth.

The Institute also supervises Uplift ceremonies, which celebrate a client race's development. Species passing milestones on their way to "adult" citizenship use such ceremonies to symbolically choose their patrons, as well as a consort race to protect their rights.

For two centuries, a committee from the Uplift Institute has been looking into the question of human origins. They dismiss as "superstition" the Darwinist notion that *Homo sapiens* might actually have achieved intelligence on its own. The committee has searched (so far in vain) for proof that humanity had a secret patron, sometime in the recent past. (In fact, by standards of Terran science, they haven't yet refuted the Darwinist hypothesis that we might, just possibly, have done it ourselves.)

The Institute for Civilized Warfare

The War Institute has, over countless millennia, organized, monitored, and enforced chivalric codes to regulate combat among the fractious clans of the Five Galaxies. With some notable exceptions, this has helped keep starfaring civilization intact, channeling the inevitable egocentric struggles of individuals, races, and clans so that feuds don't rage out of control more often than once every hundred million years or so.

> *SPECIAL ADDENDUM TO THIS EDITION: Unfortunately, the recent crisis triggered by the Earth survey-ship* **Streaker** *appears to have provoked a sudden disregard for battlefield ethics. Some radical alliances have bent or broken the traditions of conflict, hoping to seize information and reorganize the hierarchy of Galactic civilization. More honorable groups, attempting to "play by the rules," have suffered badly.*

The Institute for the Great Library

One of the oldest and most influential organizations, the Library Institute maintains a storehouse of knowledge stretching back to the dawn era of the Progenitors, covering the wisdom of countless sapient and non-sapient species—their art, science, and philosophies. Library branches come in various sizes and capacities, ranging from shipboard units less than a meter wide, to planetary centers the size of a small city, all the way to giant sector-hub archives like the one on Tanith, three jump-points from Earth. In theory, all citizen races may access Libraries. In practice, the quality of each branch unit varies according to the status of the clan that owns it. This isn't fair, but it is reality.

Terragen researchers note that employees of the Library Institute aren't always neutral, as promised. Branch units assigned to Earth ships and colonies seem small and under-programmed. Foundation agents particularly suspect the Pila race, who staff many Library functions, of slanting data to favor their Soro patrons. A major goal of each Terragen agent is to gain unlimited access to an intact branch owned by one of the senior clans. Field agents should submit full accounts of any evidence that proves discrimination.

The Institute for Migration

 The Migration Institute monitors how well each member clan cares for the living worlds it occupies. The Institute tracks millions of habitable planets, issuing leases to deserving patrons and clients for limited time spans—often for about 100,000 years. They monitor, and occasionally evict, any tenant guilty of ecological abuse. Punishment for destroying an ecosphere can include fines, loss of status and clients, or even a war of enforcement declared against the offending clan.

Worlds that have been overused are put on a *fallow list*—declared off-limits to colonize, habitate, or even visit. Fallow worlds get a minimum of half a million years, and usually much more, to heal and regrow genetic diversity. Most planets on fallow status are former colony worlds, but homeworlds can be so designated after the original sapient occupant "passes on." (See discussion of Earth's pre-contact species Die-Off, and why this shameful episode must be kept secret.)

For the last 100 million years or so, the Migration Institute has arranged for entire regions of several galaxies to lie fallow, including all major spiral arms of Galaxy Four. In part, this was due to increasing environmental fatigue, but another factor is rising friction between oxygen-breathing civilization and various hydrogen-breathing star-hives.

Because of humanity's low status, and charges of past ecological abuse, our three races of the Terragen have only been granted leases to colonize a few "recovery worlds"—planets that are rather beaten-up, or even on the verge of eco-collapse. Perhaps Earthlings got these assignments in the hope/expectation that we would fail. But humans and their clients have turned this insult into a benefit. Our colonies, such as Garth and Atlast, are bright points amid the desolation of The Ash. By healing broken ecosystems on the worlds we've leased, Earthlings are acquiring a reputation that many envy. And that some resent.

Agents should watch for attempts by our enemies to sabotage these successes and spoil our good name.

The Institute for Navigation and Trade

Trade in physical commodities would be impossible without warp drive, transfer points, and time drops. Even using these means, it is only profitable for high-value items—e.g., progressive nanotechnology, billion-year-old relics, and delicacies such as ling pears. The Trade Institute assures safety along most mercantile routes. It also maintains several data and commodity exchanges. The Galactic Price Index can take centuries to track and report, which has normally been good enough. But recent crises have thrown all markets into turmoil.

Navigation is a much more urgent and timely matter. Galactic drift can change the tidal fluxes between stars, perturbing transfer points and hyperspace shunts. This information is constantly forwarded to the Institute, but Earth only gets updates roughly every 3.2 years. If you gain access to a high-level Trade Institute database, do not hesitate to pass on the latest information.

The Institute for Progress

This small organization (only a few hundred thousand strong) promotes research and exploration. It is grossly underfunded because of the general prevailing attitude in the Five Galaxies—that most important knowledge is already known. Indeed, new scientific findings are rare, and submissions can take decades to verify. Nevertheless, the Progress Institute was said to have been established by the Progenitors, so its functions are sacred.

Ever since Earth's introduction into Galactic society, the Institute for Progress has been keenly interested in our Three Races of the Terragens, studying, among other things, how we independently developed space travel. Researchers also claim curiosity about the attitudes and morals of a "wolfling" race that managed to achieve so much without any Galactic patron to guide us.

The Institute for Foresight

This organization has functions that we've been unable to clearly determine. Among the few we *do* understand, they protect Galactic society against competition by self-reproducing machines. At times in the past, hordes of rogue automatons copied themselves by the trillions in deep space, causing enough trouble to warrant a crackdown. Today, such machine entities must apply for complicated "keys" to reproduce. Some "species" of self-replicating machine life do exist, dwelling in dark corners of space, having achieved quasi-legal status with both Oxy and Hydro civilizations.

(Field agents are urged to seek firsthand data on Machine races. Our own efforts at achieving artificial intelligence appear to follow different logical pathways than were tried in the past. This may open up opportunities, but before plunging ahead we need better data for comparison.)

All the wealthier Galactic clans contribute warships to the Foresight Institute, which uses these units to seek out "breeding grounds" and eliminate pockets of AI resistance.

Because of numerous past abuses, usually in warfare, nanotechnology is another area in which the Institute maintains a vigilant watch.

As for the more obscure activities of this Institute, our Tymbrimi friends tell us that many of these functions have to do with the interests and concerns of senior races that have "retired" or passed beyond involvement in the day-to-day struggles of starfaring culture. Some of these concerns seem vital, even urgent. Earth agents are encouraged to watch out for clues shedding light on such matters.

The Institute for Coexistence

This organization was created 1.2 billion years ago to maintain contact and relations with other orders of life, especially those eerie hydrogen-breathing races whose separate culture originates on gassy worlds, like Jupiter. This Institute helps coordinate which fallow star systems and regions hydrogen-breathers can habitate without disturbing the Civilization of Five Galaxies ... and vice versa.

(Note: Members of this Institute have lately shown acute interest in Terragen linguistics. We would very much like to know why.)

There are more than a thousand other Galactic organizations that may be called "Institutes," though none have the prestige of those described above. Also "Institutes" are created and dissolved as needed. Agents who specialize in Galactic bureaucracy will help trace these complicated structures, helping sift for dangers and opportunities. Let your advisor know if this specialty interests you!

Galactic Languages

Twelve official languages help define Galactic society. These ancient tongues—some dating back 3.1 billion years—help thousands of billions of disparate creatures to exchange thoughts, prevent conflict, and share a mostly civilized culture. Galactic languages vary in difficulty for humans and their clients. This grew evident when early translations into Anglic nearly caused disaster.

To handle the likelihood of contact with a wide range of sapients, vodor devices are built into the shoulders of all ambassadorial tunics. But remember that most vodors are based on plans found in the Galactic Library, so we can't guarantee accuracy. Field agents should have a basic grounding in at least six of the standard languages.

GAL ONE ▶ Based on pure mathematics, it uses pause and interval patterns like Morse code. It is "spoken" in many ways, with clicks, flashing lights, or bars of color. Mostly used to program "dumb" computers. (Smart machines can learn any Galactic language.) Almost any sapient species can learn to use Gal One, the *slowest* of the languages. Complex concepts are not easily passed along.

GAL TWO ▶ A popular language for bridging the gap between a great many races. It is basic, logical, unambiguous . . . and boring.

GAL THREE ▶ Favored by the Gubru and others who lack sophisticated larynx systems. Using a series of squawks and honks, it is rapidly exhausting for humans and Chimps. Dolphins seem to be good at it, though.

GAL FOUR ▶ Emphasizes echo-response, repetition, and iteration. Dolphins seem extraordinarily good at Gal Four, which makes use of primitive sonar imagery.

GAL FIVE ▶ A language of grunts and growls, spoken by the arch-like T'4Lek. A conversation in Gal Five sounds like dogs fighting on a creaky sailing ship. It is totally unpronounceable by all Terragen, though Chimps have attempted it.

GAL SIX ▶ A hissing, sibilant language, Gal Six is preferred by Synthians and Thennanin. Humans and Chimps pick it up quickly, though we speak it with a pronounced lisp.

GAL SEVEN ▶ Popular among many humanoid species and taught in all Terran schools. The Tymbrimi version of Gal Seven has an almost musical tone running behind it, linking thoughts and sentences. Ancient Terran Mandarin and its successors had similar qualities.

GAL EIGHT ▶ Comprising hoots and honks, it is preferred by the Jophur and the Rosh. Humans and Chimps can manage Gal Eight pronunciation, but suffer sore throats after a few sentences. Neo-Dolphins have a hard time maintaining focus in it.

GAL NINE ▶ Kanten, Linten, and Siqul prefer Gal Nine, with its syncopated layers. Earthlings can't come close to reproducing it. When Kanten use Gal Nine, the chiming in the background makes a pleasant—if distracting—conversational experience.

GAL TEN ▶ Brothers of the Night like this fluting, sonar-like language, well suited to underwater use. Neo-Dolphins pick it up easily. Some translated Gal Ten expressions have entered Anglic slang, mostly as curses.

GAL ELEVEN ▶ Designed to help bridge the gap with other orders of life, Gal Eleven can be transmitted by radio, laser, or psi-glyphs. It is a cautious, redundant language. Even so, it is only partly successful at surmounting the wide mental gaps between Hydrogen, Oxygen, Machine, and other orders, when misunderstandings can be dangerous. The Tandu, for some reason, seem to like it among themselves.

GAL TWELVE ▶ A throaty speech, 2 billion years old. The Soro sometimes use it, but seldom their clients. Few humans can speak rudimentary Gal Twelve and it remains unused by most clans. There are evidently hidden properties to this tongue that we do not understand. Perhaps we had best leave it alone till we know more.

The Seven Known Orders of Life

Of course you recall the nursery rhyme each Earthchild learns, to help remember the Orders of Life—**O**h **H**ow **M**y **R**eality **T**ricks **M**e **E**asily—a mnemonic that's philosophically useful as well as handy.

OXY-LIFE ❯ Beings who exist as protoplasm and metabolize with oxygen. By affinity, this includes rare species who use chlorine and fluorine. Chief attributes: fast, vigorous, ambitious lives; a subjective-sequential approach to time; proliferative reproduction strategies.
Chief political entity: the Civilization of Five Galaxies.
NEARLY ALL OF YOUR DEALINGS WILL BE WITH OXY-LIFE-FORMS. IF YOU ARE EVER CONTACTED BY A BEING WHO BELONGS TO ANY OTHER ORDER, IT IS BEST TO BREAK OFF AND REPORT THE MEETING AT ONCE TO PROPER AUTHORITIES.

HYDROGEN-LIFE ❯ Beings from Jupiter-like worlds who exist primarily as *Zhin* membranous forms and metabolize hydrogen, methane, or ammonia. Chief attributes: slow, quasi-sequential time sense; merge-division techniques of reproduction; generally heedless of individuality.

MACHINE-INTELLIGENCE ❯ Mechanical or electronic beings who exhibit digital cognizance, using nudged-muon memory processors. Chief attributes: random-access time sense; program-restrained reproductive mode; hierarchical-status sociality.

RETIRED ❯ Beings in the process of withdrawing from active involvement in the affairs of the known universe. Chief attributes: former members of Oxy, Hydro, and Machine orders all participate in the Retired Order, migrating toward regions of ever-increasing tidal force, eventually descending into the realms near black holes. Some call this a path of evolution toward the "transcendent state." Others call it nature's way of clearing away the old and making room for the new. It is generally thought that this step is voluntary, but there are at least thirty recorded cases of ascended client species "volunteering" their less-active patrons to be retired.

TRANSCENDENT ▶ Beings whose physical traits vary, but who apparently share attributes of reticence and mystery. Retired races are thought to eventually "transcend" to virtual omniscience. Some religious alliances among the Five Galaxies claim to have the support of great Transcendent forces, but their claims are disputed. The ancient Progenitors are said to have become the first and greatest Transcendent race.

MEMETIC ▶ Entities whose existence is primarily in the form of information, concepts, or psi-glyphs. Parasitic or commensal, they cannot exist without a host organism, except in the weird realm of E-Level hyperspace.

ERGOVORE ▶ Beings who metabolize energy in its purest forms—e.g., the sun ghosts who dwell in a few stars like our sun, or Ergobehems, who skate just above a singularity's event horizon.

Other Orders of Life?

According to the Galactic Library, these are the only recognized Orders of Life. There are no others. And yet, it is common knowledge that the Great Institutes have been investigating the existence of "Quantum Entities," who dwell between the known levels of hyperspace. Several other Life Orders are spoken of in rumor and legend. Field agents are encouraged to report anything they hear, no matter how outlandish or bizarre a story may sound.

*(NOTE: This section contains, in coded form, **highly classified information, to be included only in versions of this document that remain in a sealed-secure area! Do not speak of it unless trained at the Fourth Level or higher.)***

part II:

A GALLERY OF SPECIES and ALLIANCES

A Brief Survey of Galactic Star Clans—

Races and Alliances of the Five Galaxies

The following summary reports were submitted by Terragen Field Agents—and printed on paper only—in order to provide a distinctly Earthly perspective on some of the more important Galactic races, clans, and alliances. More detailed versions may be examined in your Training Center Secure Documents Room, by appointment with your instructor. In your course work, you will also tap far more detailed data from Earth's Planetary Branch Library, though this data often has a pro-Galactic slant.

Major Clans of the Five Galaxies

Most starfaring races that are citizens of the Five Galaxies seem peaceful and willing to tolerate others. But some—such as the Soro, Tandu, Thennanin, Jophur, Gubru, and Brothers of the Night—are among the most dangerous or fanatical that Earthlings have ever encountered. These receive special attention in this training manual.

WHEN ADDRESSING GALACTICS

In formal situations, start with the individual's given name, his/her/its clan name, all patron names in ascending order, and finally any client races in descending order.

a—"clan" / used to denote the species of the individual you are addressing.

ab—"patron of" / used to list the patrons of a species, in ascending order.

absu—"extinct patron of" / used to honor an extinct patron race of the species you are addressing.

ul—"client from" / used in listing clients of the species you are addressing.

ulsu—"extinct client of" / used when the sapient has a distinguished extinct client race. Rarely used in the last millennia.

chis—"patrons of" (with no singular or individual allowed in speech) / used when addressing a species that, because of a group- or hive-type mind, has no concept of the individual and needs to be greeted en masse.

Slashes are used in this guide to easily separate the race / from the patrons / from the clients. Example: "Welcome Kraat, a Soro / -ab Hul -ab Puber -ab Luber / -ul Kisa -ul Pila -ul Gello -ul Bahtwin -ul Forski."

As Dangerous as They Come—

The Star Clan of the Soro

Luber

(loo-båer) a Luber / -ul Puber -ul Hul -ul Soro -ul Kisa -ul Pila -ul Gello -ul Bahtwin -ul Forski

Having been uplifted over 625 million years ago, the Luber enjoyed one of the longest legacies in Galactic society. Luber have been inactive in the affairs of the Five Galaxies longer than most racial clans can trace their lineage. They influenced the Hul in suppressing the Data Revolt. Also, they were minor players helping the Tarseuh overthrow the "Lions." They are officially no longer part of our Galactic civilization, having retreated to fractal Retirement worlds. But they are said to emerge from the gravity tides, now and then, to look upon the affairs of their clan.

Some express contempt for the Luber, since they appear either unable or afraid to move on from retirement toward transcendence. But few dare express such thoughts aloud in the presence of a Soro!

Luber are bipedal, 2 meters tall,

Luber and Puber client at Library Institute

with wide, binocular vision on the end of muscular eyestalks. Adults mass between 600 to 700 kilos, resembling amphibious marsupials. They have three-digited hands. Proto-Lubers were thought to be swamp-dwellers. A moss-like algae might have been proto-Lubers' main food staple, scraping scum off rocks in the shallows of swamps. They now eat generic protein mash.

Your likelihood of encountering one seems nil. But if you do spot a Luber at a Senior Patron function, use extreme care. Don't humiliate our clan by committing some gaffe before one of the oldest races in the Five Galaxies.

Puber

(peu-båer) a Puber / -ab Luber / -ul Hul -ul Soro -ul Kisa -ul Pila -ul Gello -ul Bahtwin -ul Forski

Puber were uplifted over 80 million years ago, adding strength to the Luber clan. Like their patrons, the Puber have been inactive for several eons. They are bipedal, 2.5 meters tall, with binocular vision, possibly more toward the infrared. Unjointed arms end in hands with three fingers and a thumb, all tentacular. The head is prow-shaped, with vertical breathing slits. Skin is pasty, grayish yellow, tight, and muscular. Ancient records hint that proto-Puber were arboreal, a sort of tree-dwelling octopus.

Puber are more plentiful than their Luber patrons, but they too have nearly completed their move to Retirement worlds. The Soro bring a few Puber out for significant diplomatic events. Since most Terrans lack the subtle nuances of Galactic languages and protocol, we strongly advise that you retreat without embarrassing our clan.

Puber Retirement world

Hul

(hûl) a Hul / -ab Puber -ab Luber / -ul Soro -ul Kisa -ul Pila -ul Gello -ul Bahtwin -ul Forski

The Hul, along with their patrons, the Puber, have mostly retired from active participation in Galactic affairs, but this is only the latest chapter in a phenomenally long history: The Hul species has gone fallow and been reuplifted at least twice, on each occasion becoming leaders of prominent alliances of their time. According to Library records, one such "incarnated version" of the Hul had dealings with other sentients, as early as 205 million years ago. During the latest era, the Hul gained a reputation for dealing fairly with those few they considered equals, while aggressively promoting their own race and clan. Starting about a million years ago their interest began turning to "adult things," and the Hul passed on more of their responsibilities to the equally aggressive but frankly self-serving Soro.

Hul are bipedal, approximately 1.5 meters tall, with brown, leathery skin. Broad shoulders with large deltoid muscles suggest lifting/fighting was either an ancient primitive trait, or genengineered into them by the Puber. The hands have strong fingers with tiny cilia-like tentacles in between for detailed manipulative work. The tail, used for balance, was once a powerful weapon. They have binocular vision ranging to the near-ultraviolet. Sensory feelers undulate between the eyes and a ridge crest of small bony plates that runs along the top of the head, dividing the brain case into two lobes. They have breathing slits above the bony ridges over each eye.

Some evidence points to the Hul reengineering themselves after they were released from clienthood, or in each of their subsequent Uplift cycles. Internal Hul society seems to be a genetic demagoguery, with influence and riches held by individuals with the best genetically based "persuasiveness." A lottery-style infusion of randomized inheritance nodules keeps the upper echelons of Hul society from becoming inbred.

Terragen dealings with the Hul have been confined to greetings and farewells at official functions, under strict diplomatic protocols. There are abundant rumors of tension between the Hul and their clients, the mighty Soro. Field agents should carefully weigh the advantages and risks of any extended interaction with Hul.

Hul

Soro

(SO-ro) a Soro / -ab Hul -ab Puber -ab Luber / -ul Kisa -ul Pila -ul Gello -ul Bahtwin -ul Forski

---

Since their Uplift 2.1 million years ago, the Soro have striven for status with a tenacity that ranks them with the N'8ght, the Tothtoon, the Pee'oot, the Jophur, and the Poaglisis. As one of the oldest sapient races still in its dynamic phase, the Soro benefit from vast experience while retaining vigor normally long lost at such an age.

BIOLOGY ○ PSYCHOLOGY

Soro are warm-blooded reptiloid bipeds, approximately 4.5 meters in length. When young, they move much like raptor dinosaurs—young Soro are *fast,* propelling themselves on their hind legs, using their tails mainly for balance. Older Soro lose this agility; they stand by arching their backs, leaving the bulk of their bodies near the ground. Coloring ranges from dark olive green in females of reproductive age to a rusty brown for the semi-sapient males. The mouth has two tongues, and all Soro are whiskered.

While Soro vision is accurate, their hearing is quite bad. Most clients, when reporting to their mistress, speak loudly while standing directly in front of her.

Ancestral Soro were carnivores, but the sapient form is truly omnivorous, relishing a diet of exotic fruits, supplemented by meat.

The most notorious feature of Soro females, though well camouflaged, is the mating claw, a series of strong, bony digits arranged around the genitalia. More detail is hard to come by. Relevant sections in the Galactic Library have been blocked by a species taboo privacy screen. However, we believe the female Soro has a set of muscles that allow her to extend the claw, whip-like, to grab a male when she intends to mate. Soro females have been known to crush males to death with the claw, although this is now said to be rare, and some males survive five or six matings before expiring. The claw is also used for defense, and in times of stress has been known to strike the bearer of bad news.

After mating, multiple eggs gestate inside the female for about nine weeks, but in modern Soro only one egg turns fertile. Upon laying it, the female licks the egg clean and incubates it (if there is no male available to assign the chore) for the twenty-two weeks it takes to mature. The offspring, when they hatch, are voraciously hungry. Rumor tells that infant Soro are known to take large bites out of their mother!

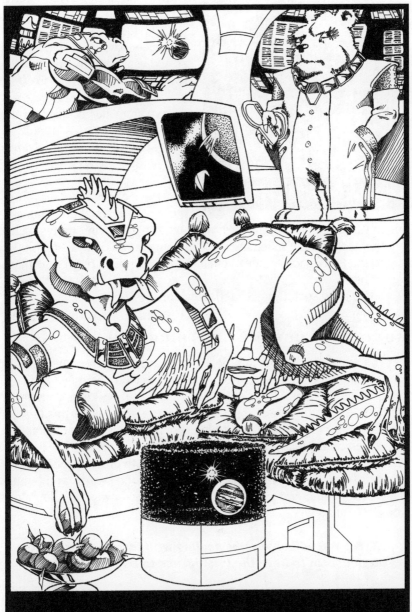

Soro with Paha mercenary and Pila Librarian

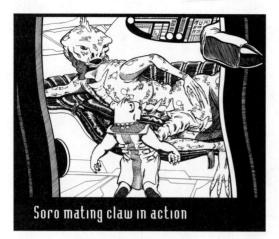

Soro mating claw in action

Growth to reproductive maturity takes fourteen years.

With technical geriatrics, Soro have been known to live as long as 400 years, but the average life span of a female is more like 180, if she is not prematurely overthrown from her position in the clan. After the stress of successive matings, males rarely live past 30.

Soro passions push them and their clients to always further both personal and clan status in Galactic society. They are masters at playing one party against another, continually scheming ways to gain control over the Institutes.

To the Soro, short-range plans involve millennia. Long-range plans last eons.

There is no such thing as a friendly Soro.

SOCIETY ◦ CONTACT WITH EARTHLINGS

The Soro race is now in a position of leadership over their prolific clan, including eight client races, three of their own and five later uplifted by their clients. Intra-Soro society is based on advancement by attrition, the battling and besting of your superior. While this has assured a vigorous ruling class, it also generates episodes of instability, which can be exploited by their enemies.

Care should be taken to address all Soro with proper Galactic titles at all times. The Tymbrimi have noted wild mood swings and temper fits. They recommend keeping at least 2 meters away from any Soro you are dealing with.

*NOTE: You will **always** be dealing with female Soro. Males do not seem to have the intelligence to boil water.*

Soro normally speak Gal Ten, a tongue of average difficulty, though it helps if you have an aptitude with Rossic or Greek. The subtlety of certain phrases in Gal Ten can elude many a first-time user. It is possible to insult an entire Soro tribe by missing the glottal stop-click at the end of a personal question, so you are advised to exercise caution.

In several negotiation sessions, Terragen agents have noticed the Soro using Pila and other clients to play roles, as in a "good cop/bad cop" routine. One client sets up a hard line, while the Soro assumes the role of the "reasonable" diplomat. There have been instances where experienced human negotiators have done quite well by exploiting the superiority assumption of Soro who grossly underestimate human skills at this age-old ruse.

Kisa

(KEE-sa) a Kisa / -ab Soro -ab Hul -ab Puber -ab Luber / -ul Pila

Kisa were uplifted by the Soro approximately 1.7 million years ago. They have remained in the shadow of their patrons, never achieving prominence in Galactic society. They seem content, doing their assigned work with a dutiful dignity.

Early Kisa evolved from an amphibian with a marsupial-like reproductive system. They are now squat-looking 1.5-meter-tall bipeds, with two trunk-like eyestalks. Around these stalks is a scattering of sensory bubbles that pick up scent, sound, and other inputs. Two optical pods face down at the ends of their eyestalks. Four-fingered hands feature long and delicate-looking digits. Originally, the Kisa diet consisted of various forms of algae, but today they are vegetarian connoisseurs.

Kisa engineer

While the Soro have positioned many members of the Pila race in the Library Institute, the Kisa have been developed into the Soro's engineering species. Most manufactured items in Galactic society are based on billion-year-old inventions. Still, the Kisa are well regarded for building, maintenance, and finding new uses for old designs.

Kisa, like their Soro patrons, speak Gal Ten. They are not antisocial, mingling and conversing well, as long as the subject matter is technical. They have shown great reluctance to express opinions about nontechnical subjects, giving some the impression they may not completely agree with Soro long-range plans. If you encounter one at a social function, be attuned to the possibility that with the right motivation and circumstances, a Kisa might be coaxed to be candid concerning Soro dealings. But beware! This could also be a trap. If possible, bring in a more experienced agent to be sure.

Pila

(PIL-a) a Pila / -ab-Kisa -ab Soro -ab Hul -ab Puber -ab Luber / -ul Pring

When they were adopted by the Kisa, 1.5 million years ago, presapient Pila lived as vindictive, warring carnivores, dwelling in a late glacial environment. Blood feuds among tribal groups raged for many generations, despite lack of significant language among proto-Pila. The Soro-Kisa clan quickly saw potential in a client whose harmless appearance masked such hard, humorless determination.

Ranging from 1 to 1.5 meters tall, Pila come from a high-gravity world, giving them surprising strength. Though they resemble mammals, the Galactic Library lists them as cold-blooded egg-layers. Their mouths are full of small, very sharp teeth. Clusters of short cilia with unknown function surround their eyes. A line of fleshy glands extend from the base of the neck to the crotch. Nearly all Pilan food is poisonous to Terragens . . . and vice versa, a limitation to be appreciated if one observes a Pila eat, a truly unsettling experience.

Pila vocal range is almost inaudible, in the near-ultrasonic, so they often wear vodors to lower the pitch. Those assigned to Earth speak Anglic tolerably well, but they prefer using Gal Five.

Of all Soro clients, Pila have proved most successful and adaptable, acting independently in dedicated service to the clan. Pila serve on the staff of prestigious Institutes. Nevertheless, many other Galactic citizens look on them as haughty little bullies, expecting more than other races of equal status, and quite often getting what they want.

Typical to their meticulous nature, Pila are extremely careful about managing ecosystems on the planets they have leased. Although this may be partly political, it is still an accomplishment. If you get a chance to obtain a copy of a Pilan eco-management manual, grab it!

Some success has been achieved with Pila by using reverse psychology—telling them you don't want something and getting the Pila to overwhelmingly insist that you do. This can work both ways. Several

Pila Librarians

key pieces of misinformation have been passed to the Soro through this method. Still, keep in mind that *all* Pila, even those sworn to service in the "neutral" Institutes, are, in one form or another, agents of the Soro. Any information they glean from you goes straight to their patrons.

During the early years of Earth's dealings with Galactic civilization, a diplomatic incident occurred, now highly classified (if you have a Level 9 clearance or higher, access file *Sundiver),* which apparently humiliated the Pila. Ever since, they have sought ways to regain face, especially at Earthling expense.

Pring

(pring) a Pring /-ab Pila -ab Soro -ab Hul -ab Puber -ab Luber

---

The Pring, despite being major clients of the high stature Pila, are socially stunted. After 112,000 years of supervised Uplift, the Pring are on their last few millennia of direct servitude, yet their Pila patrons still give them the worst jobs and assignments. The Pring have only been allowed to colonize Class A worlds—devoid of life and requiring extensive terraforming, but free of use restrictions by the Institutes of Tradition and Migration.

Terragen Library records regarding this race are woefully incomplete. But we do know the pre-sapient Pring ancestors evolved on a planet whose sun lay only two light-years from the Arcturus Maser. This environmental factor may have influenced unique features of their physiology.

BIOLOGY ○ PSYCHOLOGY

Pring average 2 to 2.5 meters tall. They have milky white skin, mottled with light gray blotches. Large lips conceal sharp, grinding plates that can be extended either for scraping or chewing. Their hands have six digits—four fingers and two opposing thumbs. As pre-sapients, their ancestors were brachiating (tree-limb swinging) foragers, moving swiftly throughout the forest canopy.

Pring speak Gal Ten through a vodor to their patrons, and to the Soro. Due to the shape of their grinding plates, once used for peeling off the high nutrient outer bark of trees, they are capable of speaking English and Anglic only with a pronounced lisp.

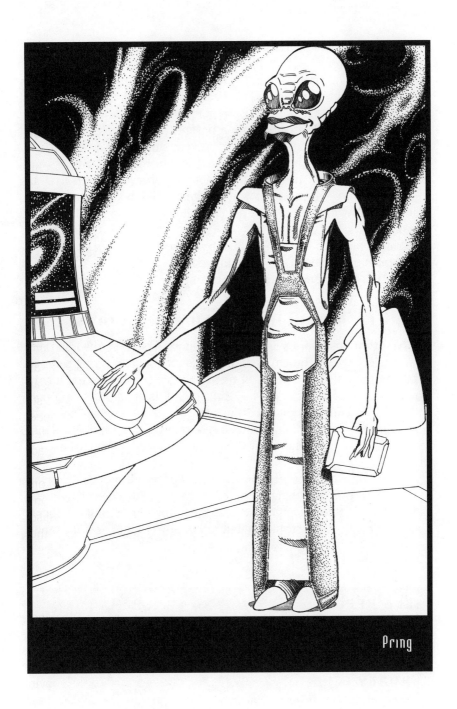

Pring

The most spectacular organic feature of Pring are their large lidless eyes, which can function as bioelectric lasers. These may have developed at first as accurate ranging systems as their ancestors leaped rapidly about 100-meter treetops. (Their eyes were cyclopic and used an organic laser range-finder for depth perception.) But the trait evolved into a weapon, and later became a potent tool for projecting optical images. Such beams are powerful enough to stun or kill.

Early notes on the bioelectric lasers come from Jacob Demwa's legendary encounters. The Pring have apparently striven hard to keep their full powers secret. There is a definite possibility that we in Earth-clan may know more about the full capabilities of Pring eyes than their Pila patrons do!

Pring reproduce by laying a clutch of three to five eggs the size of small Earth ostrich eggs, fertilized in a complex mating ritual requiring at least two males and the egg-laying female.

SOCIETY ∘ DEALINGS WITH EARTHLINGS

Tymbrimi observers suggest Pring culture has been absorbed into Pilan society with a ferocity that indicates punishment. Pring serve as thralls in the cities and farms of nearly all Pila planets except for the homeworld, Pila. The sun of Pila, an F3 dwarf, is apparently too bright for this generation of uplifted Pring. (The Pring sun is F7.) This is the reason given for continuing genetic research on the Pring visual system by the Pila, even after their Uplift license would normally have expired.

Since Pring are kept on a short leash, you must assume all conversations with one are being recorded or monitored. There have been hints of a possible underground resistance movement. Junior agents should not act on this suspicion, but report any clues to senior agents.

==

FIELD REPORT

Security Clearance: Terragen Agent Indigo or Violet levels or above
Date of Report: March 27, 159 AFC [After First Contact]
//

SUMMARY

Ever since the *Sundiver* Incident, the Terragen Council has been keeping its eye on a small race known as the Pring. As members of the Soro Clan, and indentured clients to the Pila, they would be of keen interest under any circumstances. But several unique features of Pring physiology make them worth close study, especially their organic "laser eyes."

For some time, we've known that the Pring are secretly bent on ending their indenture to the Soro Clan. Physical rebellion is hopeless, of course. But release might be achieved by filing charges of improper Uplift against their patrons before the Great Institutes. This endeavor would be difficult and dangerous, since Galactic jurisprudence is weighted to favor patrons' authority over their clients. When ready, the Pring would have to file abruptly and with overwhelming evidence.

The Terragen Council would like to know anything that might weaken the Soro Alliance, which has been so implacably hostile to Earth. Yet our efforts must be cautious. We cannot approach the Pring openly, since any association with our notorious "wolfling" clan might hurt their cause. Indeed, they suspiciously rejected efforts at contact by Terran agents in the past.

Lately, however, intelligence has come in that merits special attention from all field agents. It seems that, as part of their secret endeavor, the Pring have been attempting to invoke an *Oracle*.

About two hundred T-years ago the Pring apparently discovered an unusual region of space near their leased colony world of Pusaut. In this zone, physical constants fluctuate slightly from the norm. A search of Earth's Library branch has revealed that such anomalies have rare and unique properties. A Variance Site occasionally enables nearby observers to view alternate probability domains. It is thought that the Pring were attempting to use this quirk of space to gain oracular foresight by tapping into multiple realities.

The problem with this plan is that only certain types of brains appear to be able to "see" into a Variance Site. At first the Pring thought their holographic laser vision would be adequate. But lately they must have given up and decided that another species has the proper attributes.

That species is the Humpback Whale.

Though they heretofore rejected intergovernment contact with Earth, the Pring recently invited a pair of Earth's great whale bubble-sculptors, Solsit and Keepoit, to practice their art in a cultural exchange. The stated aim was to witness these renowned whales perform in person, and help develop a new art form: *acoustic holography.* Needing interstellar hard currency and wanting to improve relations with the Pring, the Terragen Council agreed.

The Council dispatched a small ship with Terragen Agent Brady Ahmed on board. A psi sensitive, Ahmed had orders to follow the Pring ship into the Pusaut system and observe from a distance, keeping Solsit and Keepoit under surveillance if possible. However, instead of landing on Pusaut, the Pring ship headed to an undocumented cometary outpost at the fringes of the Pusaut system. For seventeen days Ahmed observed, but could only catch brief psi glimpses of the whales. Then, on the eighteenth day, Ahmed's sensors were unexpectedly overloaded by anomalous probability waves. Without warning, about 20 cubic mictaars of space around the outpost underwent catastrophic causality inversion. All matter and energy within that zone disappeared in a silent flash of virtual translation.

Agent Ahmed reported that, moments before the ghostly disappearance, he made psi contact with Solsit. She was deeply immersed in the Whale Dream, and Ahmed figured that the acoustic interference was on the verge of success. The humpbacks were growing excited over contact they had made with some entity on the other side. A mind-spirit combination that they apparently recognized. "It felt like greeting some long-lost relative," Ahmed explained. "One you had never expected to see again."

Only then something apparently went terribly wrong—

Solsit, Keepoit, and the Pring outpost appear lost. A deep search of Earth's Library branch turned up no relevant information or references. Agent Ahmed recommended inquiring at a larger, sector-level Library branch, but the Terragen Council rejected this as costly and time-consuming. They are also cautious about alerting Pila Librarians to Pring motives. The Pring have not officially mentioned the loss of their outpost. Eager to brush over the incident, they have agreed to provide Earth with eight used but reconditioned heavy space freighters as reparation for the loss of Solsit and Keepoit, on the condition that no formal protests or inquiries be made. [Among the options to be debated in High Council: Should we use this information to blackmail the Pring into a closer relationship with Earthclan? Or would it be wiser to let it sit for a century or two?]

The Institute for Navigation has issued a hazard warning to spacers and has placed the entire region around the former Pring outpost off-limits for the next 50,000 T-years.

Gello

(JEL-lo) a Gello /-ab Soro -ab Hul -ab Puber -ab Luber /-ul Bahtwin

The Gello had a violent pre-sapiency that has continued since their race joined Galactic society 3.3 million years ago. All Gello leaders have military rank, more like warlords than politicians. And yet, this warrior race proved capable of fulfilling its Uplift contract and successfully raised a client race of their own.

Towering 2 to 2.5 meters tall, Gello have a round, sharp-toothed mouth with cilia in the corners. Four fingers are equally spaced around the palms on three-boned arms with two elbow joints on each. The leg joints are similar, ending in cloven hooves, ideal for traversing the rocky plains of their homeworld. They prefer a climate between 30 and 35 degrees centigrade, though troop movements have been recorded on planets with climates dropping as low as zero centigrade—while wearing no foul-weather gear.

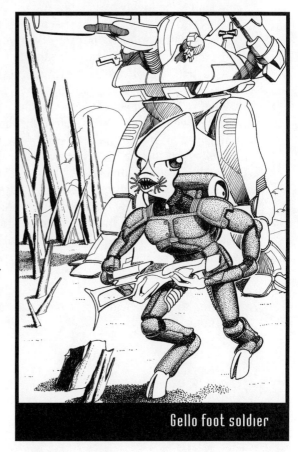

The most explicit records on the Gello are in war journals of sapients who battled against them. Cunning strategists, they are credited by the Institute for Civilized Warfare with several new variations of classic troop movements. In social situations Gello are widely perceived as hot-tempered and uncouth, though they seldom violate procedures of the War Institute. If one is acting friendly or helpful, be suspicious.

Gello foot soldier

Bahtwin

(BAAH-twin) a Bahtwin /-ab Gello -ab Soro -ab Hul -ab Puber -ab Luber

Proto-Bahtwin were intelligent gasbags floating just above the seas and forests of their homeworld, foraging and fishing. The Gello discovered them and began extensive genoforming in an attempt to make them terrestrial. To an aerial life-form this had psychological repercussions so scandalous that the Gello were sanctioned and the proto-Bahtwin were taken away from them. The Soro stepped in and finished uplifting the Bahtwin, who still seem barely to fit into Galactic society.

Bahtwin resemble a pineapple fruit cluster with an exotic air-raid siren sticking out of the top. Having lost the natural ability for flight, the entire being is supported by an anti-G harness, an inelegant "solution" that relies on an intergalactic hodgepodge of hi-technology for the species to survive at all. The whip-like tail hanging below is barbed and said to be highly toxic. They are psi-adepts, probably the strongest in the Soro clan.

Without external limbs, proto-Bahtwin originally scooped a form of airborne plankton into their lift-sacs. Now they psi-command duenna-bots to fetch and toss bags of nutrient dust for their absorption. No Bahtwin can survive without constant robotic assistance.

Being the main psi-adept branch of the clan gives them status. They are seen flaunting this before the Pring and the Paha. This prickly offensiveness may express a deeply rooted sense of frustration or inferiority. Such sibling rivalry may prove useful, playing them against other Soro Clan members.

Bahtwin are tied to the Soro in ways we barely understand. The closest comparison would be the Episiarch of the Tandu, which acts more like an insane sheepdog than a starfaring citizen race. Bahtwin psi-probing is assumed to be a part of any Soro contact. The most effective method to slow a Bahtwin probe is to form your thoughts as if you were writing calligraphy in old Japanese or Chinese. The idea of these images as if on paper seems to confuse them. They do not get the idea that such symbols can translate to Anglic or any of the Galactic languages.

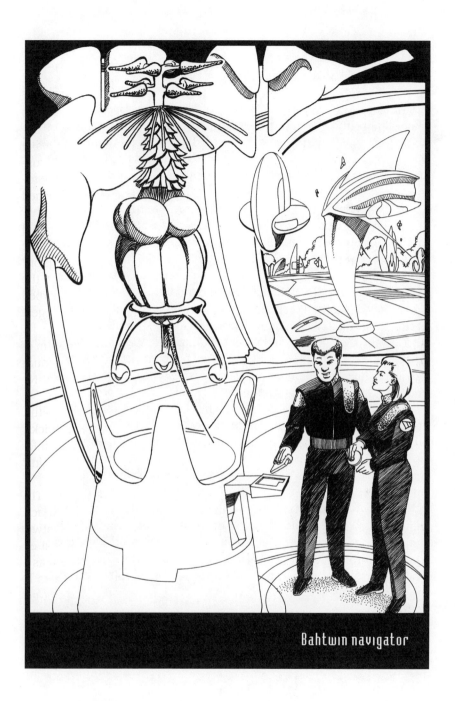

Bahtwin navigator

Forski

(FOR-skee) a Forski / -ab Soro -ab Hul -ab Puber -ab Luber

Proto-Forski were on their way to developing a peaceful culture, maintaining fruit farms in the upper branches of rain forests on their home planet, when they were discovered by the Soro. Some claim that the pseudo-avian Forski actually objected to being uplifted from the status of pets to full sapiency, but records have been privacy-sealed by the Soro.

While having a bird-like appearance, proto-Forski actually derived from cold-blooded, tree-climbing amphibians. Their feathers were originally elaborate temperature-regulating spines that could spread to collect heat from the sun or fold flat to insulate the body. Only later did conversion for flight take place. Forski biochemistry is quite alien; their blood uses heavy metal molecules to carry enormous oxygen supplies when they fly. Many Forski are "clipped," to keep them from hovering during stressful times, thereby distracting their Soro mistress.

Despite their agility and bright plumage, it was the *voice* of the Forski that brought them renown. With a seven-octave range, many can sing duets by themselves, using a split vocal box. They are the cheerleaders of the Soro clan, generally able to put a positive spin on any given situation, a trait reinforced by Uplift. Individuals who cannot contribute to overall morale are not allowed to breed.

Naturally, this greatly limits their societal potential; Forski are minor clients with no chance of becoming patrons themselves. Should the Soro pass on or go extinct, the Forski will probably have to be put under foster care.

It is doubtful that you'll meet a Forski in any role other than entertaining at official functions. If you do contact one, take advantage of the situation. Remember that the little crooners spend a great deal of time in the conference halls and bridges of Soro Clan spacecraft! Forski are said to be lousy liars and have trouble keeping secrets.

forski serenading its Soro mistress

Fair-Weather Friends—

The Star Clan of the Synthians

Pee˙oot

(PEE-oot) a Pee'oot /-ul Chelbi -ul Tharner -ul Synthian -ul Wazoon -ul Se'een -ul Klick-Klick

Pee'oot history starts 62.3 million years ago, just prior to a "time of crisis," when Galactic society became unstable. With the rebuilding, Pee'oot achieved a higher place in society than previously thought possible. Two meters tall, the Pee'oot are basically humanoid, with a high waist and double-jointed arms and legs. Their huge goggle eyes, set on each side of a snout, can rotate independently. A Pee'oot's spiral neck doesn't seem to have any bony support. Terragen biologists puzzle over how the musculature works.

Pee'oot seem tolerant of most xenotypes. Nevertheless, they are highly security-conscious. Unlike Soro paranoia, it seems more like skeptical caution. Pee'oot, and all their clan, speak Gal Six, a highly structured language, reinforcing the formality of their society. If you meet one, follow all upper-level protocols befitting sapients of their high status. They are senior patrons of an economically powerful clan.

Pee'oot ambassador with duenna-bot guard modules

Chelbı

(CHEL-bi) a Chelbi /-ab Pee'oot /-ul Tharner -ul Synthian -ul Wazoon -ul
Se'een -ul Klick-Klick

Chelbı entrepreneur dealıng wıth
human ın encounter suıt

Uplifted by the Pee'oot 38.7 million years ago, these tree-like creatures were originally ignored as an unintelligent, mobile plant life. The Chelbi had to physically surround a Pee'oot settlement, in an effort to start communicating with the star-travelers who had landed on their world. Many were burned as an "irritating weed" before the Pee'oot realized what a treasure they had stumbled upon in this new client.

Some Chelbi reach 3.5 meters, with three tentacular legs, one heavy-lifting arm, and two delicate arms per side. The "head" flares out to a 2-meter-wide disk with air-filtration fins above. They move much faster now, due to Uplift enhancements. Vertical sensors break up a "speaking band" encircling the neck area. This band functions like an old analog speaker in a 20th-century "hi-fi" system. Backed with biomagnetic nodules, it vibrates in response to neural impulses.

While Chelbi tend to be prim and formal, they are not fanatics and have been "moderate" toward Earthclan. The reign of our most ancient dynasties would seem like a passing fad compared to the stable Pee'oot legacy. Chelbi are now senior patrons and should be treated with consummate respect.

Tharner

(THAR-ner) a Tharner /-ab Chelbi -ab Pee'oot /-ul Synthian -ul Wazoon -ul Se'een -ul Klick-Klick

Eleven point seven million years ago, proto-Tharners were small, bark-eating rhinoceros-like animals when discovered by the Chelbi. It took the tree-shaped Chelbi significant time to convince the Tharners that Uplift would not cost them their individuality. Tharners distinguished themselves by avoiding any war-like conflict throughout their entire Uplift history. As their reputation grew, they excelled in mediating disputes for the Institutes of Navigation and Civilized Warfare.

Tharners were short bipeds, averaging only a meter and a quarter in height. Their beaked nose and claws on their three thick fingers were the only remaining evidence of cork-eating ancestors. Ridges ran from their oversized eyes, up over their heads. They had wrinkly gray skin like a rhino or elephant.

While the Chelbi brought ritual to the clan, Tharner traditions emphasized the importance of *patience*. They seem to have been the most tolerant of sapients, with almost a Gandhi-esque approach to any situation. One might expect races like the Soro, Tandu, or Jophur to take advantage of this. However, it seems that by playing according to proper Galactic etiquette, the Tharners were able to keep these extremists in line. Indeed, sophisticated politicians like the Soro had very productive relations with the Tharner overall.

As patrons of the Synthians, they were champions of moderation in current Galactic society. They were open and courteous when accorded the proper respect due a patron of their lineage.

However, this patience had

Two Tharner at temple

a price when many races sought help from the respected Tharner, asking protection against those fearsome meddlers, the Oallie. On behalf of Oallie victims, the Tharner filed suit before multiple Institutes. In retaliation, the Oallie unleashed a virus that nearly exterminated the Tharner, contrary to GICW rules. In return for an antidote, the Tharner accepted exile from the Civilization of Five Galaxies, moving on to the Retired Order of Life.

This time, the Oallie went too far. The Pee'oot had no trouble finding allies for counter-retribution. Soon, so many grievances had been filed that the GUI issued a Simple Writ of Extermination against the Oallie. Some say the Tharner planned it this way, all along.

Synthian

(sin-THEE-an) a Synthian /-ab Tharner -ab Chelbi -ab Pee'oot /-ul Wazoon -ul Se'een -ul Klick-Klick

Tharners found proto-Synthians 2.85 million years ago as arboreal mammals already possessing intricate tree cities led by matriarchal royalty. Foraging was a prime community activity, culminating in evening meals involving whole villages. Partly out of this gregarious tradition, Synthians are often associated with the Institutes for Uplift, Migration, Trade, and occasionally Progress.

BIOLOGY ◦ PSYCHOLOGY

Synthians are furry mammaloids, averaging 1.25 meters tall, somewhat resembling bipedal raccoons. Though shorter than most humans, it is not uncommon for a Synthian to weigh 115 kg (260 pounds).

Synthians mate in groups of three, a female and two males—one older, for insemination, and a younger one, to take responsibility for daily care of the offspring. Females and older males enjoy near-equality, dating back to their pre-Uplift lives as foraging omnivores, when sex and reproduction was a complex act, involving intricate deals among several sovereign individuals.

Their literature records quite a bit of energy and zeal. Their greatest writers have shown passion as observers of monumental events.

Synthians have four-fingered hands, with nails sharp enough to slash the throat of an enemy. Today, Synthians rarely find themselves

Synthian and Wazoon client

pushed to this extreme. They would much rather destroy your credit rating or your family name.

Synthians speak Gal Six, a guttural and sibilant-rich dialect that most humans and Chimps can handle without too much trouble. That fact, plus the ritual and formality of Synthian society, makes for a highly structured thought process.

Ironically, although they lack what we would call a well-developed sense of humor, Synthians appear to *believe* that they are very clever fellows, indeed. It can stretch your patience to pretend they are right, especially when a Synthian insists on telling one bad joke after another. But we have few enough friends in this harsh universe, so do try to smile.

SOCIETY ◦ CONTACT WITH EARTHLINGS

Pre-contact Asiatic trading families offer possible analogies for Synthian society, though one should never rely too much on Earthly comparisons. Our emissaries tend to do better after they have studied Kansai, the art of commerce in old Terragen Eastern cultures. When negotiating deals, there is much maneuvering and posturing before any business can be discussed. Yet these innocuous formalities are often important. Clients, partners, and associates use small talk to establish a tone and style for any deal that is to follow. Synthian formalities can at times seem pompous and silly when you were hoping for a relaxed, personal exchange, one on one. After all, aren't they supposed to be our friends and allies?

But patience pays off. Though they adore protocol, they seldom take deep offense over minor errors, often claiming to find our informality "refreshing." After a while, even the most stuffy host tends to relax and become quite affable. Many humans have managed to forge enduring friendships with individual Synthians.

When encountering a female in a public situation, be wary if she seems to be "flirting."

Remember that, as among the British, personal eccentricity is traditionally highly valued by Synthians. Agents note that for any given statement about Synthian culture, there will be some individual who makes it a point of "honor" to flout said convention. Try to express surprise at the individual's idiosyncracy (even if it seems rather small). You'll make her, or him, very happy.

Synthians have little military power, though some think their commercial fleet could be converted into a formidable force. It is through their sophisticated intelligence service that they seem able—and willing—to be helpful. Some of our most successful agents have forged relationships with Synthian counterparts—without trusting them completely.

In any event, remember that the deepest Synthian instinct—to survive—tends to outweigh friendship, almost every time.

Their help can only be expected when it seems likely they'll be backing a winner.

Wazoon

(wa-ZOON) a Wazoon / -ab Synthian -ab Tharner -ab Chelbi -ab Pee'oot

Arboreal Wazoon were found on their homeworld by the Synthians 420,000 years ago. Finding a proto-species so similar to their own early development, Synthians quickly nurtured the tiny clients into a folk possessing both substance and subtlety. Wazoon have quietly maneuvered behind the scenes of Galactic society for generations, doing favors and intelligence gathering for their patrons—and for others willing to pay.

Wazoon are small and tarsier-like, rarely over 50 centimeters tall, covered with a soft down, ranging from light tan to a speckled rust coloring. Their two most notable physical features are their sight and hearing. Their incredibly large eyes see a spectrum similar to ours but with considerably more sensitivity to ultraviolet. This is nothing compared with their hearing. There are documented cases of Wazoon hearing quiet conversations all the way across a large room, during loud parties. Their four-fingered hands have large, sandpaper-like pads on the ends. The feet have a heel spur that hooks over tree limbs.

The little Wazoon are fiercely loyal to their patrons and their clan. They have demonstrated innovation and assertiveness above and beyond what one would expect from such a tiny client. Inferences in Synthian document crystals imply that Wazoons are the intelligence gathering network for their patrons.

Wazoon and patron on starliner

The Star Clan of the Thennanin

Tothtoon

(TOTH-toon) a Tothtoon / -ul Rosh -ul Kosh -ul Wortl -ul Thennanin -ul Paimin -ul Rammin -ul Ynnin -ul Olumimun -ul Garthling

Seven hundred and forty million years ago, proto-Tothtoon existed as a community of 3-meter-wide, shallows-dwelling octopi. After adoption, their patrons found that the new client race had been exploring *pure mathematics* for ages. Even before they were fully sapient. Tothtoon made important contributions to the wisdom contained in the Galactic Library.

They have gone through six different stages of personal reengineering over their 240-million-year history, most recently transforming from armored octopods, with chitinous shells, into helium-filled jellyfish, gliding the air currents of their Retirement worlds. (Thennanin have installed nutrient stations at strategic locations around these planets.) A Tothtoon's arched gasbag flares out to four flat arms with feeder cilia on the underside, covered by nutrient-absorbing pleats. Though technically retired, they are active enough in Galactic affairs to advise younger races in their extended clan.

Today's Tothtoon float in "contemplation groups" of twenty to a hundred, arranging complex patterns, like gatherings of sperm whales, hovering at altitudes from 600 meters to 4,600 meters. Some think Tothtoon communicate among themselves by psi-casting in groups.

After the recent alliance between the Thennanin and Earthclan, Terran officials were invited to meet some of these near-transcendent beings. The apparent scope of their philosophy eclipsed anything our scholars hope to achieve in millennia. Recording devices came back filled to capacity—and excruciatingly hard to interpret.

Terragen expedition monitoring Tothtoon tribe

Late one night, a member of our delegation noted multicolored lightning in the distance. He realized there were no clouds. And the lightning flickered across the sky in complex geometric patterns.

Rosh

(roosh) a Rosh /-ab Tothtoon /-ul Kosh -ul Wortl -ul Thennanin -ul Paimin -ul Rammin -ul Ynnin -ul Olumimun -ul Garthling

Rosh were found and uplifted by the Tothtoon 641 million years ago. They ran in herds, like tool-using buffalo. Surviving notes made by a Tothtoon poet marveled at the sight of 200,000 trunks raised in greeting above a vast plain of grass.

Rosh are 1.75 meters tall. Their massive teardrop bodies start with an elephantine trunk. The feet have large toenails along the front, and claws—probably for defense—on the outside. Two arms look minuscule compared to the body, but are more powerful than a human's. Ancient herd dynamics still echo in their society. Leadership used to be won through physical combat to the death. Today, Rosh choose their leaders in complex rituals, testing the fittest Rosh in Olympic-style games.

Rosh were founding members of the Abdicator Alliance, having witnessed the departure of the Tarseuh and the six elder races, interpreting the event as a mystical evolutionary process. Like their client's clients, the Thennanin, they have a reputation as fair, yet firm, never backing down on basic Abdicator tenets, perhaps hoping the Great Ghosts will come back through them or a client.

Though technically retired, Rosh seem to like a good party. Rosh delegates attend gala events, often seeming relaxed and informal. Nevertheless, these are *senior* patrons with high visibility, so you are advised to use all proper protocols. If possible find a Tymbrimi. They have extensive interaction with Rosh at social functions and seem good at striking the right note of easygoing respect. Business dealings are best passed through a Thennanin or Wortl.

Rosh meeting with a Tymbrimi Institute official

Kosh

(kaash) a Kosh /-ab Rosh -ab Tothtoon /-ul Wortl -ul Thennanin -ul Paimin -ul Rammin -ul Ynnin -ul Olumimun -ul Garthling

Kosh and Wortl arriving at formal dinner

Kosh date back 80 million years, to the time of the Revolt of the Data, when they apparently volunteered to be temporarily altered into biological data-storage units, to save information then being lost to memetic plagues. After stable neural/passive storage units were created, they resumed their journey of Uplift.

Kosh are generally an odd shade of light lavender, reminding one of a purple cabbage. They feel to the touch like aloe vera cactus. 2.5 meters tall, they have a bipedal vertical musculature with alternating large and small tentacles arranged around the upper torso. The "head" consists of two flattened quatraspheres. These may be eyes or other sensory organs. Contracting and expanding the two flexible, boneless legs gives the Kosh a rolling gait like a sailor on a moving ship.

Kosh have gone to elder status, just short of retirement. But instead of retreating to some out-of-the-way world, hidden and protected by their clients, Kosh take a Zen-like attitude, immersing themselves in Galactic culture and observing anything they can be invited to watch. They show up at the oddest times. One Tymbrimi sage likened it to having your great-grandfather insist on coming along to the mall, claiming that he won't get in the way. It takes some getting used to.

Wortl

(WART-l) a Wortl /-ab Kosh -ab Rosh -ab Tothtoon /-ul Thennanin -ul Paimin -ul Rammin -ul Ynnin -ul Olumimun -ul Garthling

Kosh uplifted the Wortl 39 million years ago. As new citizens, Wortl helped coordinate the final hundred millennia of the Union for Self-Esteem, gaining respect for their earnest efforts. "Responsible as a Wortl" is a catchphrase.

They are 2.5-meter-tall bipeds with slim cylindrical heads. Faceted eyes bulge from either side, two-thirds of the way up their heads. The neck features gill-like breathing slits. Hands are rounded cones with eight mini-finger tentacles at the ends of multiple-jointed arms. Wortl wear robes covering most of their bodies.

Sometimes Wortl appear to play on their reputation for patience by deliberately showing signs of annoyance. Wortl still have great influence with their clients, the mighty Thennanin. They are obviously going to play an important role in the ongoing Uplift of Garthlings (Gorillas), so getting to know them better is suddenly a high priority.

Agents that recently met with Wortl found them more stuffy than the affable Rosh and Kosh. Others claim they are serious, but as open-minded as any Galactic. We can only hope for the best.

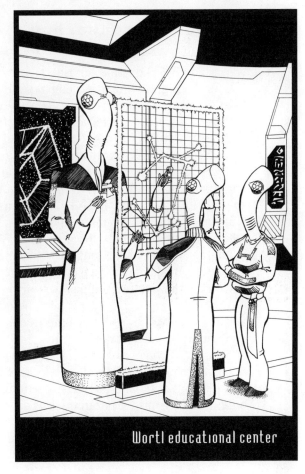

Wortl educational center

Thennanin

(the-NA-nin) a Thennanin /-ab Wortl -ab Kosh -ab Rosh -ab Tothtoon /-ul
Paimin -ul Rammin -ul Ynnin -ul Olumimun -ul Garthling

Thennanin were uplifted 33 million years ago by the Wortl, a peaceful but highly manipulative race, well versed in Galactic law and its consequences. Having a keen sense for battle and tactics, Thennanin originally became the Wortl's enforcement arm.

Since their release from clienthood, Thennanin have proceeded with a methodical enhancement of their role and power base within Galactic society. This has not been the rapid, fanatical expansion of the Soro or Tandu. Yet, Thennanin leadership has resulted in more planets being deeded to their Tothtoon Clan in the last 10 million years than any other Uplift family.

BIOLOGY ○ PSYCHOLOGY

Thennanin biology most closely resembles reptiles, although warm-blooded like some dinosaurs. They are bipeds, averaging 2.75 meters in height, with short, elephantine legs. A ridge-crest extends from just between the eyes to the upper back of the neck, serving simultaneously as a filter for aiding in breathing, a means of regulating body temperature, and a sexually selected display. On the elbows of a male Thennanin's powerful arms are spikes that can be flexed like bird feathers into position to preen the ridge-crest, though in the pre-sapient past it may have served other functions. They clean the elbow spikes with baleen-like teeth along the insides of their mouths. Their main breathing and communication is done through a series of vertical gill-like breathing slits in the thick neck. From this, we can conclude that their native world must have had a complicated atmosphere. Something made breathing a complicated process!

Thennanin coloring ranges from light tan to a reddish chocolate brown. Ridge-crest colors have been noted in a wide variety of colors, and may be dyed in some fashion trends. Coloring does not seem to correlate with social status.

Thennanin have two sexes and mate for life. Home and family are of major importance to Thennanin culture. Females lay clutches of one to three eggs at regular intervals timed to the year of their homeworld, but nowadays only two or three eggs are viable during the course of a lifetime.

Many parts of the Thennanin diet are edible to Terragens. In fact,

Thennanin General Buoult on the command deck

toasted brill, a sort of avian crayfish, is a delicacy not to be missed at Thennanin state functions.

"Stuffy" is the term most Terragens use after meeting a Thennanin. This is obviously an oversimplification of the sense of spirituality and ritual that pervades Thennanin culture. They are not easily angered, although they do have deep passions about matters that concern them most.

SOCIETY ◦ CONTACT WITH EARTHLINGS

Thennanin culture is framed by many Wortl rituals and ceremonies, instilling traditions, honor, and a resistance to change.

THE ABDICATOR ALLIANCE

The Wortl, and the Kosh before them, passed on the tenets of the Abdicator Alliance. Abdicators date back approximately 600 million years, to the Tarseuh Incident. The "Lions," a powerful alliance of races, dominated and ruined vast numbers of ecosystems through unchecked colonization.

The Tarseuh convinced six elder races, all thought to have "passed on" to a higher plane, to help stop the "Lions." Afterward, the Tarseuh and the six elder races vanished forever.

This has led to the concept of ethereal beings, "Great Ghosts," who are possibly related to the Progenitors, guiding events in the Five Galaxies. Legend speaks of Great Ghosts entering and imbuing themselves into pre-client species who are uplifted and eventually become powerful patrons, protecting and counseling the rest of Galactic society. The closest parallel in Earth culture is the Buddhist concept of an enlightened spirit who returns to the world in a new body in order to help ease the way for others.

Only in this case the messianic visit comes through an entire, sainted *species,* come back to guide all sapient life. This parallel makes the Abdicator philosophy one of the easiest Galactic belief systems for Earthers to understand. This does not necessarily make it *attractive* to us folk of the Terragens.

Thennanin have shown general neutrality toward the Terragens, neither helping nor hindering our efforts to find a place in the Five Galaxies. They did vote against giving humans patron-level status, and applied to adopt us "for our own good." But this was apparently done without hostility. It is interesting to note that a moderate-level Thennanin official has attended nearly every Terragen event they were invited to, while many other clans and races continue to snub us socially. This seems to show an open interest in what we "wolflings" are up to. Though there may be an underlying agenda that we know nothing about.

> **UPDATE FOR THIS EDITION: Now we see the sudden, unexpected advent of an alliance with the Tothtoon Clan, and its vigorous leader-race, the Thennanin, bringing valuable aid when we were hardest pressed. For the reasons behind this alliance, see page 14.**

Paimin

(PIE-min) a Paimin /-ab Thennanin -ab Wortl -ab Kosh -ab Rosh -ab Tothtoon

Paimin were accidentally discovered in a rain forest on their homeworld 1.9 million years ago, during a routine planetary survey. The planet had been left fallow for 5 million years. Paimin are 1.5- to 1.75-meters-tall bipeds. Their heads are reminiscent of an elephant because of the prehensile trunk. Paimin heads flare out into a large neck shield covering puffy air-slits. Coloring ranges from light taupe to lime green. Like their patrons, Paimin prefer Gal Six, but many are fluent in five or more Galactic languages. One recent emissary to Earth spoke almost perfect Anglic.

Paimin seem well adapted to serve as delegates for the Thennanin. They portray a stoic poker-face, then suddenly appear puppy-dog friendly, often taking you off guard. Alliance or no alliance, watch yourself around Paimin. They are smarter than they look.

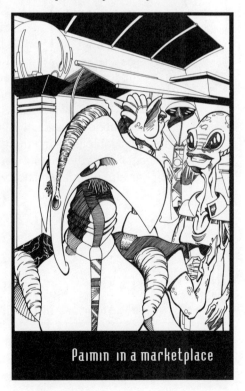

Paimin in a marketplace

Rammin

(RAM-in) a Rammin /-ab Thennanin -ab Wortl -ab Kosh -ab Rosh -ab Tothtoon

Thennanin found the proto-Rammin languishing around the fading oases that dotted their desert homeworld, which had been written off

Rammin "walking the dog"

by the Galactic Institutes as an ecological "lost cause." During Uplift, these hardy beings became the Thennanin's warrior caste. But when their indenture expired, they petitioned to pass this duty to the next client in line, the Ynnin.

1.5-meter-tall bipeds, the Rammin have two elbows on each arm. Their hands have two strong fingers and three opposable, dexterous fingers. Forward-facing optical sensors spread across the face. It is suspected these "see" in many different wavelength bands.

Rammin have been a low-key presence in Galactic affairs, tending to live somewhat apart from the rest of Galactic society, congregating in low-density star clusters. They are notoriously resistent to control by outsiders, even their patrons. They exhibit a languid yet stubborn fatalism that may seem charming—if you're not trying to accomplish something with them.

Agents are advised not to fly with Rammin pilots. Every one of them has already made peace with its maker.

Ynnin

(JIN-in) a Ynnin /-ab Thennanin -ab Wortl -ab Kosh -ab Rosh -ab Tothtoon

Ynnin were uplifted 850,000 years ago by the Thennanin, who found a culture akin to a Neolithic trading society. Though already possessing a primitive form of writing, the Ynnin were nevertheless decidedly pre-sapient. The Thennanin chose proto-Ynnin for Uplift over other more promising candidates on planet Ynn. It seems that Ynnin were chosen *because* of their herd-oriented, nearly herbivorous heritage.

The Ynnin nursery world is currently held as an ecological preserve, pending extinction of the proto-Ynnin control population.

Both male and female Ynnin have a kangaroo-like posture and gait. Proto-Ynnin lived in moderate-sized herds typically containing twelve to forty females and young. During mating season, matrifocal herds dissolved as males competed for prime territory, displayed, and gathered temporary brood herds. As omnivores, proto-Ynnin would break open rotten logs and eat grubs, along with any scavenged meat they chanced upon. But most nutrition came from mixed scrub and grass. Ynnin armor evolved from fatty tissue, quilted between two layers of rhinoceros-like skin.

Like their Thennanin patrons, Ynnin seem earnest and fanatical, but scrupulously fair. Like many newly uplifted races, they can also be incredibly idealistic. Ynnin have become excellent ecologists, an aim that permeates their culture. So above all, do not even hint at Earth's tragic Die-Off secret. We cannot afford even a rumor to undermine this crucial source of help.

Ynnin ecological survey crew

Olumimun

(o-LUM-i-mun) a Olumimun /-ab Thennanin -ab Wortl -ab Kosh -ab Rosh -ab Tothtoon

The youngest direct Thennanin client race, Olumimun were up-lifted 520,000 years ago, when crude circular villages of proto-Olumimun were observed with "highways" leading from all four compass headings to a central cooking pit. Daily, the proto-Olumimun would set a fire and wait. Soon, one or two animals would stagger in from a nearby wild herd and blindly drop into the pit. Olumimun apparently "wished," and the animal—always a creature past its prime breeding age—just showed up. They also wished each "guest" to have no pain. (These behaviors, while moral and sophisticated, should not be mistaken for true sapiency. They had evolved over lengthy periods, and were less culturally than biologically determined.)

The Thennanin quickly petitioned to adopt these promising new clients.

Olumimun body proportions are hidden under all-concealing robes. We suspect they have been reengineering themselves since achieving release from their indenture, and are not ready to show off the finished product. Olumimun heads are shaped like art-deco hood ornaments. They have two sets of eyes, both below pronounced eye-brow ridges.

Though the Thennanin tend to dislike psi-powers, they desperately needed to have a race of adepts in their clan, or face profound disadvantage against foes like the Tandu. For this reason, the stolid, amiable Olumimun were a treasured find. Never intruding their mind-probes where they feel unwanted, Olumimun are now the psi-guards of Thennanin Clan, especially on warships or at state functions. Unlike the Tandus' Episiarch slaves, the Olumimun are completely sapient, exercising conscious restraint in their use of power.

Some feel that if the Great Ghosts are going to return to the Galaxies, they would choose the most excellent vessels they can find. The Olumimun apparently plan to be those vessels.

Olumimun manager running orbiting drydock

Garthling

(GARTH-ling) a Garthling /-zor Human -ab Thennanin -ab Wortl -ab Kosh -ab Rosh -ab Tothtoon

---

Garthlings are descendants of Earth Gorillas who were illegally transported to the colony on Garth. About forty years ago, a group of humans and neo-Chimps began an unsanctioned attempt to uplift an experimental population of Gorillas, violating a Terragen pledge to leave the species fallow for 1,000 years. The attempt was thwarted—half finished—when the Gubru invaded Garth.

Through a bizarre series of circumstances (that remain somewhat shrouded, even now) this combination of calamities actually worked to the *benefit* of Earthclan. One result was adoption of the Gorilla species by the legendary Thennanin. This made the Thennanin our allies at a crucial point in the latest Galactic crisis, perhaps saving Earth from imminent conquest. Since it appears we would have lost all rights to Gorillas anyway, this seems a positive outcome. At least we will have some voice in how they are uplifted by the kindly (but stiff) Thennanin.

Like their Terrestrial brethren, adult Garthlings average 400 to 500 kg. Because their Uplift is just beginning, there have been minimal changes so far, principally the posturing of enlarged frontal lobes and expanded sign-language ability. Preliminary observations show a perception of the grand scale of Galactic society. They show promise of becoming interesting people, with a distinct worldview all their own.

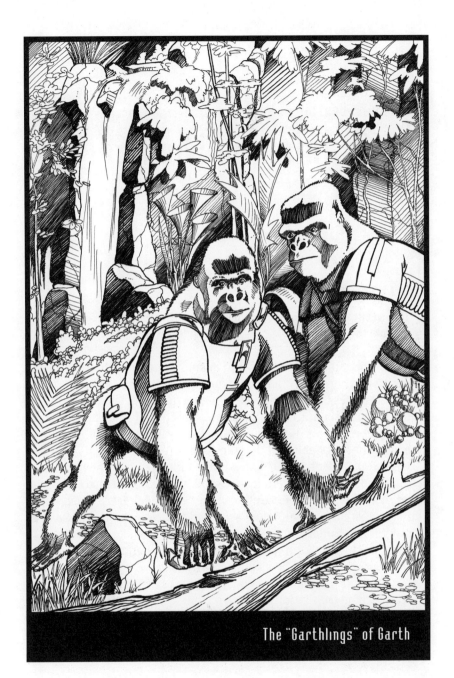

The "Garthlings" of Garth

An Unwilling Destiny—

The Fonnir and the Norruhk

Fonnir

(fon-NEER) a Fonnir /-ab Zhosh -ab Plkhosh -ab Plkseuh -ab Tarseuh / -ul Norruhk

Their appearance has led some agents to assume that Fonnir are similar to Earthly sloths. But closer interaction proved these short, six-limbed creatures to be quick-witted, with a quirky, devil-may-care attitude. This may seem to contradict their tight-laced Abdicator Alliance upbringing. However, if they feel that they have the Great Ghosts on their side, they probably feel that they can do no wrong.

Do the psi-adept Fonnir know something special? Their recklessness extends to using alternate-probability drives similar to those favored by the Tandu. More cautious races shy away from these wildly unpredictable devices, although schematics have been in the Galactic Library for millennia. Fonnir seem quite content to take the risk.

Their strange mixture of fanaticism, daring lightheartedness, and single-mindedness may be as alien as anything we have encountered. Fonnir have not yet felt the legendary Embrace of Tides—the call to retire close to the gravitational pull of a white dwarf or neutron star—yet they have ambitions to leapfrog ahead, hoping to achieve a *transcendent,* immaterial state beyond the cares and demands of our order of sapience. Who knows? If they succeed, it should provide an interesting spectacle.

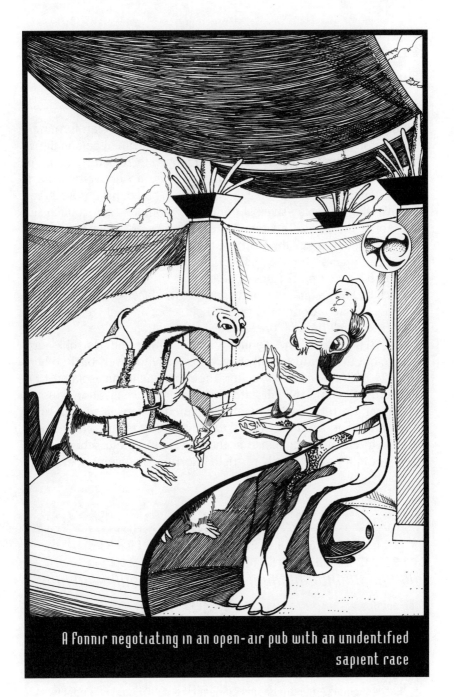

A fonnir negotiating in an open-air pub with an unidentified sapient race

Norruhk

(NOR-uk) a Norruhk /-ab Fonnir -ab Zhosh -ab Plkhosh -ab Plkseuh -ab Tarseuh

Proto-Norruhk were a herd-like species, with each clan forming a psionic group-mind. There seemed to be little individual personality in any single Norruhk. This has not changed much in 70,000 years of Uplift. Individuals are generally shy, though they do understand basic sapient concepts and are capable of speech. The Fonnir enrolled their Norruhk clients in extensive psi training to promote their singular talents. About the size of a Great Dane, Norruhks are covered by slick, black fur. Quadrupeds, the Norruhk have front paws with highly manipulative "tingers," but they still require robotic help to do fine work. They are not adept mechanics or artisans.

Norruhk have a quadrilaterally symmetrical face with four jaws and four eyes situated around the skull. Their sexes are only recognizable by other Norruhk through pheromone identification.

For 70,000 years the Fonnir found uplifting the Norruhk easy enough, but the creatures still show a tendency to revert back to herd mentality. Without constant cultural reinforcement, an isolated Norruhk herd will completely discard all trappings of civilization within a generation. Norruhk have a highly structured society, filled with ritual and strong conduct codes, partly to control this reversion tendency, but also to ensure compliance in their patrons' "grand scheme" (see below). Fonnir have severely restricted Norruhk involvement in Galactic society.

===

AN AGENT'S REPORT ON AN EXCEPTIONAL EPISODE INVOLVING THE NORRUHK

///

Dear Jacob,

Thank you for the holos of our old place. You've done wonders with it. Renee and I are glad that it is in good hands.

As you can see from the attachments list, this has been a busy month. Busy and extraordinary.

"Extraordinary" hardly begins to describe it. If I absentmindedly sent you any requests for a transfer off Deemi, tear them up! The things I've seen and done this month more than make up for the tedious trip out here, the raw landscape, and the meteorological excesses of a botched terraforming job.

Here it is in a nutshell: For a few weeks, it looked as if humanity was on the verge of becoming the de facto patrons of a sapient species that has been around for ten times longer than recorded human history.

One of them is trying to curl up in my lap as I dictate this...no mean feat for a creature the size of a Great Dane. Young Ghoo-Ooor'p is a female, critic-caste Norruhk. The chims at the spaceport call them *tar elks*, which fits: They're quadrupeds, slender and graceful, with astonishingly glossy black fur and a body temperature in the high forties.

Hmm...if your trip to Tanith to submit a final neo-Dog genotype went off as planned, you've met Ghoo-Ooor'p's kind: Many of Director Emzhahkunna's staff are Norruhk. The Institute for Uplift is the only place you're likely to find the creatures, outside of K?kakk and a few backwater colonies.

To continue: Three weeks ago, a Fonnir-registered ship slid into our obscure little colony system, trailing five ghostly alternate-probability versions of itself. (One of which had pink...well, no, I think I'll save that for our next meeting, over strong drinks!) My staff tells me this is the signature of a ship using soft-quantum tunneling, an FTL technique so esoteric that our tiny branch Library squawked. The crew transmitted legitimate diplomatic credentials, however, and so were granted permission to land, at Port Shipley. They had already arranged for accommodations at Hal's, the local eatee hotel, by the time Commander Ecklar and I arrived. We introduced ourselves, gracefully accepted the honorific-laced greetings due a patron species, and improvised a welcoming speech suitable for the clients of a clan founded sometime in the Cretaceous.

Frankly, we were at a loss of what to do next. Our guests—fifteen of the lanky creatures, wearing no signs of rank or status—had still not disclosed the nature of their visit. Hyung spontaneously suggested a tour of the town, requisitioning five private grav sleds and sending a Class Scarlet emergency signal to the mayor's comm slate. It was an excellent move; in addition to giving my staff time to find out more about our guests, we'd get a chance to show off what we've done with the sorriest piece of real estate in the sector. The Norruhk spent hours poking their four-jawed, four-eyed faces into valleys and around some of Deemi's unique erosion spires. They seemed particularly interested in the school and Academy, and in the tiny neo-Dolphin colony that's been mucking about in Atrocious Bay.

The mayor was in full regalia and had a speech ready by the time we got to City Hall. The Norruhk supplied polite praise for our efforts on this

Norruhk "pups"

abused planet, but failed to respond or rise to the bait when Hizzoner offered to assist them in whatever business brought them to Deemi.

It was the Norruhk's turn to surprise us. They invited me, Lee Hyung, the mayor, Director Monteiro of the Academy, and Lasmer Dart to a banquet at Hal's.

[An aside: Harold Stubbs, the hostel's manager, came to my office the next day, describing the frantic preparations he and his staff had to go through, arranging a multispecies soiree. He then handed over a Commerce Institute transfer plaque he'd been given by the Norruhk as payment—good for nearly 1,500 minutes of priority access time at the Tanith Sector Library! In return, he asked us to reimburse Hal's, plus a 30 percent gratuity for his staff. It sounds quite fair, after what they went through.]

As customary at this type of affair, the two delegations exchanged initial greetings, ate separately, then rejoined to exchange pleasantries and loosen up over mild intoxicants. One of our hosts read a long appreciation, praising Earthclan for overcoming our handicaps, for our efforts to reclaim ravaged worlds, and for our two fine client species—Chimps and Dolphins. Then, after the reading, they presented us with... the Orphans.

That's what the legation called the group of slender young Norruhk who stepped through the door at that point. Indeed, Ghoo-Ooor'p and her five companions have no recent memories of their parents. But the delegation's official story—that the youngsters' home arcology was undermined in a storm and collapsed, and that they need our help to take care of the homeless unfortunates—did not ring true. Yes, large portions of K?kakk's ecosphere are going to pot; and yes, most Norruhk and their near-senescent patrons cower in a few dozen arcologies. There is even a precedent for endangered client populations to be transported offworld and placed under the protection of another patron race. But the Fonnir are ancient and respected and have many favors due them. Moreover, the Norruhk have a few colonies of their own where the youngsters could have been better cared for.

We were suspicious but played along. We were given nutrient synthesizers, health maintenance equipment, and a stack of data slabs with Norruhk parenting information. Then, before we could even adapt our bathroom plumbing for the new arrivals, the legation of adult Norruhks left!

Imagine a ship of humans landed on an alien world and gave over half a dozen of their children to the care of strangers. Oh, there could be plausible circumstances when it might happen—all of them terribly desperate. We were filled with unease.

Fortunately, our new charges did not seem upset over being abandoned on a backwater "wolfling" colony. They fell in love with our staff almost immediately, and we with them. Each youngster selected one or two chims or humans as mentors and teachers, refusing to be separated from them. This was hardly a burden, since young Norruhk are fascinating creatures, yet perfectly content to watch you work between bouts of answering questions.

They gracefully submitted to Dr. Pomm's physical examinations, resulting in our second surprise of the week. Each of the youths has, attached to the normal analogues of ovaries or testes, a compact protein-based computer implant! According to the medical databases we were given, these contain the genetic patterns of several million individual Norruhk. In other words, these youngsters aren't random refugees, after all. They were specially equipped to establish a new branch of their species.

With the help of Tymbrimi Ambassador Kullerum's staff, we set out to discover all we could about the august Fonnir and their last surviving client race. Most Library entries are dense but unhelpful, intended primarily as tributes to the long, successful career of a conformist patron race. But by reading between the lines, and paying a small fortune in Gal-Coins to a visiting Lesh merchant, we discovered the following:

Fonnir are psionic adepts, and have spent the last dozen millennia working on what Abdicators refer to (loosely translated from Gal Three) as "The Final/Absolute/Sufficient Spiritual/Ontological Conundrum." They feel on the verge of solving it. If Abdicator claims are right, they will thereby achieve a transcendent, immaterial state beyond the cares and demands of our order of sapience.

It all sounds appropriately creepy and mysterious. Just the sort of thing ancient Galactics are supposed to do, when they get old. So what? How does this concern the Norruhk? Other than the fact that they will achieve manumission and freedom 30,000 years ahead of time?

Ah, but there's the rub. Norruhk—who are powerful in psi themselves—appear to play a vital role in the Fonnir plan for apotheosis. They aren't mere catalysts. Like the unlucky servants of ancient Terran kings, they are doomed to *accompany* their masters into "the next life"!

The dear creature now dozing on my lap is about five years old. If returned to K7kakk, there is a good chance she'll live to witness the end of the Fonnir and Norruhk as corporeal species. She may become part of something strange, terrible, and wonderful. Many Galactics would see this as a boon bestowed by wise and loving patrons, a shortcut to a state that most achieve only after millions of years.

Perhaps most Norruhk think this is just fine... but a small faction ob-

viously disagrees. And they chose Earthclan—a symbol of youth and vi-
tality (to the races that don't hate us)—as agents of deliverance. The
Fonnir never chose Third Stage Uplift Consorts for the Norruhk, so by
some interpretations of Galactic Law, humanity might assume this role,
and become the Norruhk's patrons in all but name, when the populations
of K?kakk and its colonies transcend.

It tears my heart to say it, but this trust in Earthclan was based on
romantic misconceptions. We aren't capable of such a duty. Not now.

I do think we could do a creditable job of raising these remarkable
creatures to age nineteen, when Norruhk become physically mature and
their mental powers manifest. But then, each of the three castes—crit-
ics, synthesizers, and seers—develop different psionic talents, none of
which we have any experience dealing with. More disturbing, the open and
flexible personalities of childhood harden during adolescence into
stereotyped patterns appropriate to the individual's caste. The wonderful xenophilia that makes young Norruhk natural diplomats turns into
something rather...well, kinky. (The full details are in Dr. Pomm's report.
Briefly: Norruhk can only interbreed with those of another caste. Adults
consider anyone with a personality different than their own to be of another caste, and therefore desirable!)

The ingenious Fonnir developed a way of life for the Norruhk that includes elaborate social rituals, a rigorous education, psionic training
academies, along with strict moral and ethical codes. These are not an
imposition: They are necessary. Our Lesh contact described what happens
to Norruhk populations that do not adhere to this scheme: Left to themselves, the creatures quickly shed civilized norms, abandon their cities,
and eschew all but the simplest tools. After a generation in the wild, they
gather in herds guided by telepathically mediated mass-minds of subhu-
man intelligence. In other words, they are far from ready to graduate
from client status. The task of guiding them further may take extraordinary skill.

Assuming they don't all accompany the Fonnir to transcendence,
that is.

When it became clear that we could not help these poor creatures, we
arranged through Ambassador Kullerum to contact what remains of the
Fonnir diplomatic corps. Another ship is on its way here, even as I
speak—a ship staffed by loyal Norruhk and one actual Fonnir. A full report
on their visit will be on its way by priority cast as soon as possible.

My staff and I are resigned to seeing the Orphans go. Kullerum com-
miserated with us in his own style, by pointing out the delightful absurd-
ity of it all—that a client of one of the oldest patron races trusted its
children to "wolflings" who seem scarcely able to defend their own clan.

His admission that even the adroit Tymbrimi could not handle adult Norruhk made me feel a bit better. It may well be that no one can help these creatures escape the fate their patrons decreed.

While we had to give up a chance to become step-patrons, Earthclan may get something out of this. We're spending lots of time with the alien youngsters before they go. Renee and Stefanson plan a week of cultural activities—games, lessons, and dramas presented by the settlement's human children—to teach the Orphans about human history and the values of Earthclan. They learn fast, these alien kids, and they don't forget. Perhaps in a hundred years, when the Norruhk loyally follow their patrons to another sapient order, they'll bring pleasant memories of us with them.

Anyway, it never hurts to have friends in high places....

I remain your devoted friend.

Hefni Emshwiller,
Hitten Station, Deemi Colony

Not Our Brothers—
The Star Clan of the Brother

Nighthunters

(nighthunters) a Nighthunters /-ul Brothers of the Night

Most Library photos of this extinct race appear stiff and formal, showing Nighthunters in stately robes. The attached picture, passed on to us by a Tymbrimi scholar, is one of a few hinting at their true nature. It was found in a recording device about a million years after it was dropped by one of the Nighthunters' victims. From image enhancement, we see Nighthunters were probably 2.5 meters tall and 4 meters long. It is suspected that almost every bodily fluid of Nighthunters was poisonous to most of the sapients of the Five Galaxies.

They were uplifted by unknown patrons approximately 211 million years ago.

They raised up the Brothers of the Night, hoping for a good challenge. Nighthunters are now extinct.

Brothers of the Night

(brothers of the night) chis Brothers /-absu Nighthunters

Brothers (a term used for both males and females) were uplifted by the Nighthunters, who made up their own splinter sect of the Awaiter Alliance. The Nighthunters took this brutal species of cunning pre-

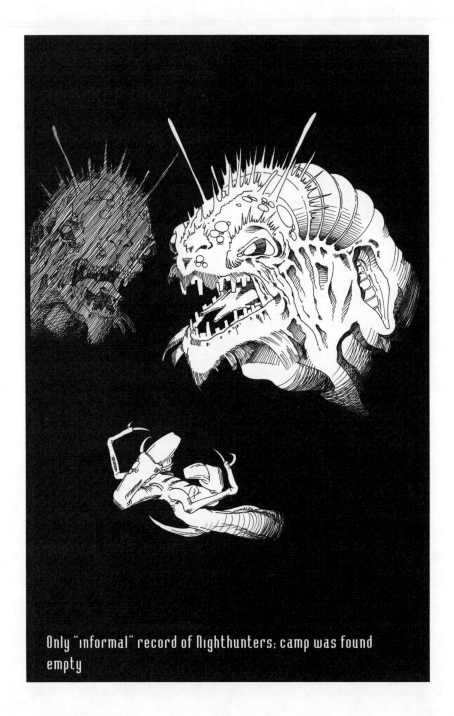

Only "informal" record of Nighthunters; camp was found empty

sapients and fostered them into sophisticated and formidable beings with an unfortunate proclivity for forming fanatical cults. There are hints that the Nighthunters' intent was to create decent competition (or prey) for secret predatory rites. According to this rumor, the Nighthunters promised the Brothers ascension to full liberty on the day they managed to conquer their patrons.

Apparently, the Brothers succeeded.

As pre-sapient creatures, Brothers lived in large packs, glued together by elaborate social rituals; packs would split, violently, whenever these rituals changed. "Dissenters" were killed or driven away to form new packs. Records hint that entire Brothers' cultures would vanish when the balance of power would swing to a new, larger pack of "dissenters."

Since Uplift, this trait continued in a tendency of Brother communities to dissolve amid spirals of heresy, orthodox recrimination, and fragmentation. While these fractures can be exploited by enemies, the schisms seldom last very long. Under external pressure, Brothers drop their feuds as quickly as they erupt and engage in frenzied ceremonies of joyous forgiveness.

During the present crisis era, large numbers of these passionate beings see themselves as "Holy Warriors," chosen to cleanse the Galaxy of infidels. Others style themselves as defenders of civilization and protectors of the weak. From experience, both kinds seem equally dangerous.

BIOLOGY ○ PSYCHOLOGY

Brothers are six-limbed, warm-blooded amphibious carnivores, with powerful upper arms for fighting and crude manipulation. Delicate lower arms are used for detailed work. In water, the upper pair cover the lower, which are pressed into indentations along the upper torso. Thick legs lock together with a swimming tail that wraps around both. The tail's outer edge has minute razor-sharp serrations, capable of separating an opponent's limbs. Some consider this product of controlled evolution to be the deadliest killing machine in water since the great white shark. In an evolutionary parallel, the mouth of a Brother is structured almost identically to a great white's, set into its chest, close to its stomach.

Motives are hard to define in a species once intrinsically devoted to killing. Brothers are ambitious and highly chauvinistic, rather than simply xenophobic. They even possess an odd (and chilling) kind of empathy. With what seems almost like gregarious eagerness, they seek out strangers and thrive on meeting "zaga," which unnervingly translates as "fresh meat." Perhaps that phrase is rooted in a still-unquenched inner drive to understand the ways of their next kill. Certainly Galactic

Brothers surfacing in arcology colony

society has not squelched these undertones. But layers of protocol and a passion for procedure keep the Brothers from actually eating outsiders. Most of the time.

The result is a race of individuals who are highly manipulative in social situations, always attempting to maneuver themselves like a chess game to be won or lost. They are at their best one on one, which can sometimes lead to dynamic conversations about ideas. But these can quickly devolve into argument. When a Brother decides to "convert" you to some True Path, the proselyte may cling to you relentlessly. In extreme cases, your options will boil down to fleeing...or converting the Brother to some less obnoxious creed. (It has happened.)

Few sapients accuse a Brother of being boring. Very few would risk falling asleep in one's presence.

SOCIETY ⚬ CONTACT WITH EARTHLINGS

Within any particular community or sect, Brothers generally form hierarchical societies akin to militant religious orders. Brothers dedicate their lives to a production or industrial brigade, an intelligence team, a monastery, or a military unit. Individuals advance on acts of merit and tests of ideological correctness. Members of an order treat each other with much consideration and a genuine, but restrained, "brotherly" affection—as long as everyone piously supports the current brand of orthodoxy.

Library records show that Brothers do not have permanent mates or family units. Individuals are given permission to mate (usually with someone in their existing unit) by committees of matriarchs. Offspring are turned over to a host group, similar to a kibbutz or mocha'deen. Three to seven elderly raise up to two dozen young.

You should avoid dealing with any Brother without advice from someone with seniority and experience. This is not to ensure proper Galactic decorum—Brothers seldom attack other sentients over mere social transgression. But many of them react badly to disagreements over fact or opinion. In other words, they dislike being told they are wrong. This makes anything but basic social exchanges problematical. If you do get into a disagreement, make sure it's in a public place. The presence of lots of witnesses can keep things from getting deadly. Most of the time.

Star Clan of the Tymbrimi

Krallnith

(KRAL-nith) a Krallnith /-ul Brma -ulsu Caltmour -ul Tymbrimi -ul Tytlal

As one of the oldest sapient races, it is obscure why the Krallnith haven't transcended or passed on with others from the same era. It is suspected that many Krallnith are hidden on fractal worlds, slowly reinventing themselves for what they consider their next stage of evolution. Like the Luber, they are able to resist the Embrace of Tides long enough to emerge from retirement for brief visits to star lanes of the Five Galaxies.

Having modified themselves several times over their 711-million-year history, Krallnith are now 8-meter-tall tripods. Two eyes gaze from between each set of legs as massive as large oaks. A mass of tentacles three meters long surrounds a downward-facing mouth. Tymbrimi have a visual record of a Krallnith throng on a fractal world habitat, racing across an artificial prairie. The sight of hundreds of 40-ton tripods thundering along, at 35 kilometers per hour, is awesome to behold.

The Tymbrimi are quiet about Krallnith thoughts and motivations, and from Krallnith writings seen in Tymbrimi archives, they seem philosophically detached from material world concerns. Withdrawal by the Krallnith from Galactic society happened after the eradication of the Caltmour in the suppression of the "Lions." After the Tarseuh victory, at the heavy cost of the Caltmour, the Krallnith seem to have spent eons evaluating the meaning of life.

A couple of Terragen agents have had the privilege of meeting

Senior Krallnith greeting visitors

Krallnith (with all the official protocols and supervision by the Tymbrimi and the Brma) and found them to be pleasant and patient, as if we were very small children.

Brma

(bier-MAH) a Brma /-ab Krallnith /-ulsu Caltmour -ul Tymbrimi -ul Tytlal

Almost 81 million years ago, the Krallnith found the Brma homeworld an ecological nightmare. The proto-Brmese were breeding and grazing uncontrollably, destroying an Eden-like environment. The Krallnith's first objective, on receiving the Brma indenture, was to ingrain the "tread lightly on the land" caveat.

Brma resemble 2.5-meter-tall bipedal insectoids, with large, compound eyes. Coloring ranges from orangish brown to lime green, with pale lateral stripes. Their four genders are alpha male, alpha female, beta male, and beta female. The two females have preliminary intercourse to fuse RNA, making a reproducible ovum. Males perform in a similar manner, generating a spermatophore—a capsule encasing hybrid spermatozoa during reproduction. The alpha female has a birthing pouch on her back where infants are carried for thirty-six months.

Some of the eccentric attitudes embraced by the Tymbrimi originated with the Brma, who see new blood and ideas as key to rejuvenating stagnant Galactic society. Though semiretired, the Brma have stayed active. They helped save us after the NuDawn disaster and have kindly lent their presence to every Uplift ceremony for our Dolphin and Chimp clients.

We owe them. Big-time. If an agent gets a chance to do the Brma a favor, don't hesitate.

Brma overseeing Uplift ceremony

Caltmour

Proto-Caltmour were found in almost a pre-Cambrian ooze. They seemed poor candidates for sapiency and their Uplift by the Brma was almost disallowed. The Uplift Institute offered a 2,000-year trial waiver, which proved more than adequate for them to reach Stage 1. Some think their speedy Uplift was rooted in irreverence toward pompous Galactic society.

Tymbrimi with his Caltmour patron [ancient record]

Caltmour were originally 1-meter-long pentapods living in algae-covered tide pools. (Their superficial resemblance to the Krallnith appears to have been coincidence.) Two main visual sensing arrays ran along either side of the sleek head, with cilia and food manipulation tentacles below. The pentapod body structure bent upward, turning two of the legs into arms, with shoulders broadened for heavy work. After initial genetic modifications, the Brma decided that the Caltmour were well suited for intellectual work. They were rapidly released from indenture and allowed to seek clients of their own.

Tymbrimi speak fondly of their lost patrons, having learned from the Caltmour to perceive the universe as a vast and mysterious cosmic joke. They hope the Caltmour found a good punch line.

Tymbrimi

(tim-BRIM-ee) a Tymbrimi /-absu Caltmour -ab Brma -ab Krallnith /-ul Tytlal

HISTORY

Tymbrimi have a well-deserved reputation as practical jokers and innovators. Library records indicate that the Caltmour (now extinct) manipulated the proto-Tymbrimi for this trait, deliberately enhancing an already puckish nature to help counterbalance the conservative, priggish society that now reigns in the Civilization of Five Galaxies. When the Tymbrimi became patrons, they in turn continued this tradition by uplifting the impish Tytlal.

BIOLOGY ⇨ PSYCHOLOGY

The humanoid Tymbrimi are mammal-like, shorter and slighter than an average human. Females have six breasts and a marsupial-like pouch capable of large litters, though nowadays they seldom let themselves give birth to more than one child at a time. Tymbrimi thighs are shorter than those of humans and their calves longer, adapting them better for climbing than for long-distance running.

The Tymbrimi face is at once both familiar and alien, with an arrangement of eyes, nose, and mouth similar to humans. Tym skin is more translucent than ours, though colorations vary widely. Tymbrimi usually have light body hair with a Mohawk-like ruff of fur running from between their eyes to the base of the neck. On either side of the head, from the temples to behind the ears, a series of tendrils form almost a halo. When communicating with other Tymbrimi, they not only speak a dialect of Gal Seven, but also form *glyphs*—a form of telepathic, poetical expression that envelopes and enhances the exchange of meaning. While empathic humans are known to sense these auras, only general impressions come through. For the most part, we are blind to this rich element of Tymbrimi life.

Like their patrons, Tymbrimi look at the universe as a cosmic riddle. Moreover, they believe the punch line of a joke is less important than the telling. The odds are overwhelmingly against them maintaining sanity in a fanatical universe, so why not at least enjoy the ride?

Many humans misunderstand the Tymbrimi art of *Takahin'tuf,* believing it consists of an endless predilection for practical jokes and tomfoolery. This all-too-common interpretation strays far from the subtly complex philosophical basis for a central passion of Tymbrimi life. Novice Terragen agents are urged, therefore, to immerse them-

Tymbrimi ambassador

selves in Wolfe's *The Art of Surprise,* and the virtual-reality masterpiece *Gotcha!* It is important for Earthclan representatives to grasp the strangely skewed sense of fair play underlying *Takahin'tuf.* One is never supposed to lay a trap for someone without leaving a path of escape—one that the victim is fully capable of seeing. One that he or she could easily use, by simply questioning some overused assumption.

An observed example happened about a year ago at the Library on Tanith. A single Pila librarian was singled out as a prime target. The Tym organizing the prank had fifty of her associates approach this particular Pila and ask for research on doomsday devices. They then requested information on Retirement fractal worlds, and the different procedures for "ascending" or "transcending," the implication being that the Krallnith were *way* overdue to transcend and that these individuals were going to find the fractal worlds and hasten the process along. At any point the Pila had the opportunity to note that it's impossible for one individual to cause another to transcend. Also that it's logistically impossible for so few sapients to destroy dozens of fractal worlds, doomsday device or not.

Instead, the Pila took information on the requesting sapients and turned it in to his Brma supervisor, in an attempt to save tens of millions of senior race members' lives. The supervisor, who had prior experience with such pranks, kept things from getting out of hand by exposing the joke.

Inflexibility—considered a virtue by many Galactic races—draws only contempt from a Tym. Bearing this in mind, we can be grateful they are stalwart allies. By the same token, however, it is probably a good thing that Tymbrimi aren't running the universe.

SOCIETY ○ CONTACT WITH EARTHLINGS

Tymbrimi society is a loose democratic communism in which leaders are appointed to ad hoc posts with one foremost rule: If they actually crave the job, they are disqualified. The closest Terragen equivalent would be jury duty. Leaders accept this arrangement out of a sense of responsibility, aware of their difficult place in Galactic society—plus a prevailing attitude that life consists of nasty jokes dealt by an immature universe. To a Tym, the worst thing a person can do is to whine about bad luck. (Terragen agents should bear this in mind. When accompanying a Tymbrimi, it is far better to make fun of ill fortune than to act bitter about any bad breaks that befall you.)

Tymbrimi have imparted a similar sense of the absurd to their clients, enlisting the Tytlal as coconspirators in several pranks they unleashed on mighty empires such as the Soro and the Thennanin.

Needless to say, this trait seems hardly calculated to increase Tym odds of long-term survival. Their explanation: Why worry?

CONTACT ⚬ DEALINGS

Tymbrimi have been among the most open and helpful of any Galactic civilization, perhaps because they see Earthclan as the biggest jest yet against a stuffy cosmos. Yet, in spite of this, you should be wary. Not out of fear, but because few Tym will pass up a chance for a "good" poke at a friend. While this may seem acceptable in closed company, it won't help your standing with *other* Galactics to suffer a public pratfall. In today's political climate, it is doubtful the Tymbrimi as a whole would do anything to endanger our alliance of underdogs. But *individually* we are fair game.

Remember, they are friends and they seem almost human. But they are aliens.

Tytlal

(TITE-lal) a Tytlal /-ab Tymbrimi -absu Caltmour -ab Brma -ab Krallnith

Tytlal have only been free clients for a thousand years. Yet Tymbrimi admit that many of their greatest pranks were initiated by their impish clients. An average Tytlal is approximately 1 meter tall, weighing about 20 kilos. They resemble upright otters with perpetual smirks. Silky brown fur covers their bodies.

Tytlal have a freewheeling democratic society. Massive information blitzes precede collective voting on any topic imaginable, with each voter getting a multiplier determined by a "give a damn" formula, or how deeply the individual cares. (This can be complicated if one attempts to go to dinner with a group.) Unlike their Tymbrimi patrons, Tytlal have a marked taste for acquisitions and a verve for capitalist enterprise.

As a field agent you will find Tytlal most helpful in information gathering. Often, they ask only that you trade a new gag or punch line. Sometimes you can get one to help you on a dare.

Tytlal exhibit a great curiosity about anything Earthling. They get a kick out of old Three Stooges recordings, which explains a lot.

Tytlal at the ready

Life Can Be Strange—
The Star Clan of the Jophur

P o a

(POA) a Poa /-ul Jophur -ul Sarrphor -ul Phasheni -ul Dorrvi -ul Voam-Voam

Patrons of the mighty Jophur, the gentle but hasty Poa appear to be ending their 13-million-year citizenship and preparing to enter the Retired Order of Life. Their history tells of many impulsive decisions that went badly...and as many that somehow worked out for the best, winning them many friends. But after letting the enigmatic Oallie interfere in Jophur Uplift, the Poa finally realized the high price of carelessness. They decided to forgo guiding other proto-sapients.

Not counting antennae, Poa are 2 to 2.25 meters high and 4 to 5 meters in length. Each resembles a sleek snail with an immense foot surrounded by hundreds of tentacles. 2-meter-long antennae are probably sensory organs. Coloring varies wildly from tans to fluorescent magenta, suggesting they have the ability to communicate through color changes.

As they prepare to retire to the fractal worlds, Poa are seen rarely in Galactic society. It is doubtful you'll ever come closer to one than these pictures. But if you do, try courteously to get the creature's attention and interest in hearing the story of Earthclan. If, by some chance, these honored beings decided to champion our cause, it could make a difference!

Poa and Jophur with proto-Traeki

Jophur

(DZOU-fur) a Jophur /-ab Poa /-ul Sarrphor -ul Phasheni -ul Dorrvi -ul Voam-Voam

Jophur are among the most alien oxygen-breathing species encountered by Earthlings. Visually and biologically closer to plant life than animal, they were gene-engineered extensively by the gentle Poa 7 million years ago, in part because of prodigious Jophur abilities to process and recall information. But the resulting sapient creature showed a notable lack of ambition, frustrating their patrons.

Known for making hasty decisions, the Poa turned to the notoriously conceited Oallie for help.

The result? In a startling transformation, Jophur became one of the most profoundly egotistical, ambitious, and amoral races in all Five Galaxies.

BIOLOGY ○ PSYCHOLOGY

Jophur are among the few sapient species one might call "cultivated." Individuals consist of a series of stacked sap rings, each a semiautonomous organism capable of surviving on photosynthesis or saprophytosis (mulch eating). Each ring has rudimentary intelligence, plus a suite of talents to contribute to the whole stack—manipulative, sensory, neurological, or digestive. (Imagine a human whose arms, legs, and other organs all had "minds" of their own and argued among themselves each time a major decision must be made.)

When assembled properly, by a team of skilled adults, a normal stack of roughly fourteen rings includes one for propulsion, two for manipulation, one or two sensory rings, a voice ring, several cognition and memory toruses, plus two unspecialized rings serving as food-processing plants. Propulsion and manipulative rings start basically the same, but on assembly they respond to hormonal changes. Nodes on the outer edge grow into arm-like tentacles or root-like legs. The average fourteen-ring Jophur is about 2 meters tall. Jophur speak Gal Eight or Gal Two.

Millennia ago, the Jophur called themselves *Traeki*. Overall intelligence was high, but these composite beings lacked the purity of focus needed for quick or ambitious action. Traeki did not originally propagate in vats. Instead, they would either catch and combine wild rings or else create special toruses in a process of *Vlen-budding*. A blister would form about halfway up the side of a Traeki, crack open, and spill

Jophur meeting Linten and Terragen agent

forth new rings. In this way, selective memories and talents could be passed on to an offspring.

Impatient with the loose Traeki personality, the Poa called in harsh Uplift experts, the Oallie. Beyond starting vat reproduction, they also introduced a "Master Ring" to every stack of toruses. This dominant entity coordinates production of appropriate hormones and uses neuroelectric shocks to prod other rings into concerted action. The resulting *Jophur* were a new class of being.

SOCIETY ◦ CONTACT WITH EARTHLINGS

Jophur are members of the Obeyer Alliance, a sect believing that spiritual presences guide believers' destinies. They received this faith *not* from their Poa patrons but from their Uplift consorts, the Oallie. Among themselves, Jophur engage in fierce mutual competition, punctuated by episodes of "mingling," when egotism is put aside.

Jophur psychology is mysterious. Their relentless self-interest and driving ambition seem frenetic, as if overcompensating for their Traeki past. If you have direct contact with a Jophur, attempt to have other patron-level beings present—though *not* a member of the Abdicator Alliance, such as the Thennanin. It will do you no good to get mired in age-old disputes between dogmatic followers of obscure doctrines that no Earthling understands.

Sarrphor

(SAR-for) a Sarrphor /-ab Jophur -ab Poa /-ul Phasheni

Jophur found the proto-Sarrphor half a million years ago in freshwater swamps. Though lacking sapiency and technology, they had developed a complicated caste system with the strongest family assuming a caliphate. The Jophur left this system in place.

Sarrphor are 2.5-meter-tall centauroids whose eyestalks rotate independently, registering mostly infrared. The brain is not protected by a skull, but sits on a tray-like frame covered with tendons. Two flexible boneless arms end in pincers with fine-manipulation cilia. Their mouths are a series of horizontal slits, each with its own set of vocal chords, piped from a single lung. Currently the Sarrphor are diligent clients, but history implies they have unusual forcefulness—call

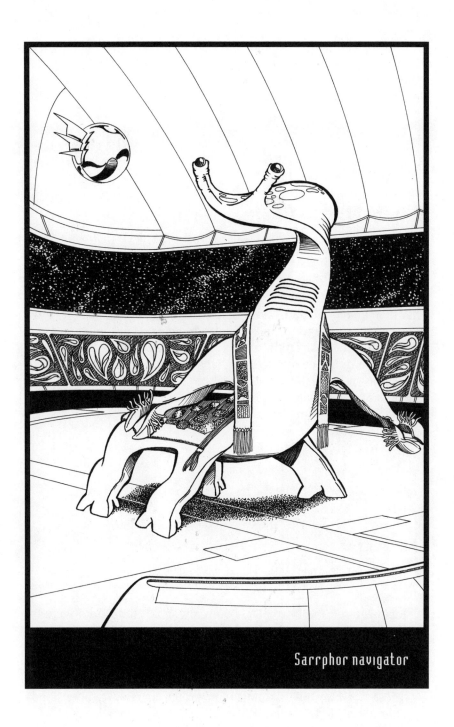

Sarrphor navigator

it "spunk." The fierce Jophur have had to renegotiate their patron-client relationship at least twice. One can only suppose that something about the Sarrphor gives them an advantage. Try to find out what it is.

Phasheni

(fash-EN-ee) a Phasheni /-ab Jophur -ab Poa

The Phasheni were uplifted 587,000 years ago by the Jophur, partly to mitigate the extreme stance (even by Galactic standards) of the Jophur Clan and to mitigate bad feelings over the Oallie episode. In other words, they were bred to be likeable and to present a "kinder and gentler" side to the Civilization of Five Galaxies. As outward representatives of one of the most powerful clans, the Phasheni appear to have created a small niche for themselves wherein they have minute amounts of freedom. It may be possible to leverage this knowledge so watch out for any signs that a Phasheni may be disgruntled with their oppressive masters.

Dorrvi

(DOOR-vee) a Dorrvi /-ab Jophur -ab Poa /-ul Voam-Voam

Jophur raised the Dorrvi 563,000 years ago. Proto-Dorrvi were the rogue elephants of their homeworld, pummeling anything in their way. The Jophur first liked their smell, being pheromone-oriented. Their physical strength has actually been toned down to allow safe interaction with other Galactics.

These are big, hulking guys with proportionally itty-bitty hands. Don't arm wrestle with them. Little else is known, biologically.

Being the Jophur's right-tentacle men has benefits and disadvantages for the Dorrvi. The Dorrvi lately (within the last 10,000 years) have been used by the Jophur as the trading branch of the clan. The

Phasheni litigator on a break

Dorrvi traders going through Customs

Jophur probably think that the huge Dorrvi present a less threatening, more appealing appearance than the multicolored, flaccid ring-stacks of a Jophur merchant prince.

Voam-Voam

(voam-VOAM) a Voam-Voam / -ab Dorrvi -ab Jophur -ab Poa

Dorrvi found the Voam-Voam 223,000 years ago as grazing herbivores. 2.75 meters tall, they have a triangular body ending in twenty-two tiny feet. The bilateral tentacular arms end in suction-cupped fingers. The head arches forward in a huge proboscis, splitting to two nostrils in front of the mouth. Large eyes give the Voam-Voam bird-like vision. Voam-Voam appear withdrawn and enigmatic, even though they are now free from indenture. They have autonomy to run their own affairs, so long as they provide vigorous help to the Jophur in their Galactic ambitions.

Voam-Voam tourist

Not Easy Being Green—
The Kanten and Their Star Clan

Siqul

(SICK-quil) a Siqul /-ul Linten -ul Kanten -ul Nish

Siqul were uplifted 1.2 billion years ago. Most records about them are little better than notes and legends. They are bipedal and gangly, at almost 3 meters tall, with large optical sensors that are technically not eyes. They "see" a wide range of the electromagnetic spectrum, from the lower gamma radiation at the high-end spectrum, into the area of radio waves. Their five-fingered hands have radial symmetry.

Having long delayed their entry to the Retired Order, the Siqul seem in no hurry to leave Galactic society, preferring a slow-paced existence as casual hobbyists, floating from one mild interest to the next, letting the Linten handle all responsibilities. They avoid most formalities.

Archeology is an especially favored Siqul hobby, slowly filling gaps in ancient history that predate the memnetic plagues. They enjoy inviting younger sapients along on their digs, so there are opportunities to work with these Galactic historians. Just remember to speak slowly, and be prepared for long-winded answers.

Siqul archeologist

Linten

(LIN-ten) a Linten /-ab Siqul /-ul Kanten -ul Nish

Siqul found their Linten clients living in a proto-agrarian society, with an already well-developed image of the world as Mother Planet. This led to key positions for uplifted Linten in the Institute for Migration and the Institute for Foresight. Bipedal Linten average 2.5 to 3 meters tall and 400 to 500 kilos. Flexible finger-tentacles have fine hairs along the inner palm, capable of detecting minute textural and temperature differences, comparable to Terran Kirlian sensors. Some biologists suspect a Linten can act almost as a polygraph, detecting the flush response in some humanoids and correctly reading their intentions.

Linten society seems to resemble an early Terran Buddhist monastery. They pride themselves as teachers in the ways of universal unity. Many Earthling pilgrims travel to study with Linten masters. However, Linten perceptions can be quirky, even untrustworthy, as if they sometimes see levels much deeper than we do, and get distracted from the topic at hand.

Kanten

(KAN-ten) a Kanten /-ab Linten -ab Siqul /-ul Nish

The Kanten have a remarkable place in Galactic society. Since rising from proto-sapience 22 million years ago, guided by the Linten gardeners, Kanten gained prominence as some of the fairest mediators in space, achieving key positions in several Galactic Institutes. Kanten-led negotiations settled a number of key wars in recent millennia, saving three starfaring races from extinction.

The Kanten originally developed mobility to avoid the cyclical droughts on their home planet. As evolution continued, forests of Kanten migrated across whole continents. A proto-society later grew out of cooperation in developing vast irrigation systems. By discovering and adopting these unique pre-sapients, the Linten achieved one of the most remarkable feats in Uplift history.

Linten biologist lecturing

BIOLOGY ○ PSYCHOLOGY

Adult Kanten stand up to 3 meters tall. The first Terragen agent to see one blurted that it resembled a mobile stalk of broccoli. Fortunately, Kanten have low egotism and don't easily take offense. Silver balls spread across the upper foliage of an adult Kanten. Arrangements of crystal shards cluster at their apex, thought to be part of the Kanten speech apparatus. They have retractable claws in their root-pods—sharp and incredibly hard.

Among themselves, Kanten use Gal Nine. Even Dolphins have little luck speaking it fluently. Kanten are adept linguists, however, and seldom need translators.

Among the most congenial species in Galactic society, Kanten are always attempting to look at the big picture, seeking balance. Perhaps a plant-based species has a more harmonious connection with nature, perceiving the connectedness of all things. While this orientation seems attractive at one level, it can also be frustrating to a short-sighted Terragen agent, who must seek answers quickly, dealing with events taking place over days, even minutes.

SOCIETY ○ CONTACT WITH EARTHLINGS

Kanten society developed into genuine communism where everything in their society is pooled for the use of all, similar to Marxist fantasy-prescriptions from pre-contact Earth. (Those prescriptions seem to work just fine ... in another species.) With a Gaia-like attitude, Kanten almost eliminated the singular in conversation, until they had to restore it for interaction with Galactic culture. They tend to be unbiased observers and can be especially useful to have as a witness when you deal with unfriendly Galactics. However, don't expect much active assistance. A Kanten's sympathy is nice, but it's less effective in a tight spot than a well-aimed blaster.

Nish

(NISH) a Nish / -ab Kanten -ab Linten -ab Siqul

The proto-Nish were originally thought to be a highly mobile tree-fungus by their Kanten and Linten discoverers ... until a visiting Tymbrimi *dared* a Kanten scholar to attempt communication. To the

A Kanten "wallflower" at formal function

surprise of everyone—especially the puckish Tym—there resulted a resonance indicating substantial pre-sapient potential! Thus began one of the more amicable and surprising tales of Uplift.

Innately shapeless, Nish generate pseudopods for movement and manipulation as needed. Most extend two legs (though they are generally not symmetrical), often with a balancing tail or forward prop. Nodules or pipes protrude from odd places, probably serving as sensors. Skin texture is reminiscent of a sponge. Reproduction occurs by a kind of culturing process, using bits of DNA from a partner as a starter, like the yeast in sourdough bread.

Highly creative, Nish are fine artisans. But they are also solitary creatures, associating with their kind primarily to mate. They are a bit more gregarious among individuals of other races. In a forest setting, you may pass a Nish without noticing. Pay attention to where you are walking.

Nish holographic sculptor

Your Worst Nightmare—

Star Clan of the Tandu

N˙8ght

(N-āt-ght) a N'8ght /-ul Tandu -ul Acceptor -ul Episiarch -ul Incrementor
(Note: The pronunciation of "ght" in this case is a glottal catch in the throat, which sounds like a cross between a cat with a furball and a fish jumping out of water.)

According to Inheritor teachings, N'8ght are the race most closely related (genetically) to the Progenitors. Other alliances reject this, asserting that false records were inserted during the memnetic plagues to reinforce disreputable family lines. Whoever their actual patrons were, the N'8ght were among the most aggressive species to populate the early Galaxies. They seem bitterly frustrated that the Progenitors did not leave clear evidence that they are rightful heirs and owners of the Five Galaxies.

A note about the coalition organized to suppress the "Lions," of which the N'8ght were members, refers to several races having to forcibly stop the N'8ght after they destroyed sapients not directly associated with the "Lions."

Originally, after Uplift, the N'8ght defied the "live lightly on the land" tenet. Expanding from world to world, they decimated ecologies filled with potential Uplift clients. Later, faced with threatened retribution, they appeared to repent. In place of the destroyed environments, N'8ght built beautiful, intricate worlds. Indeed, having three intelligent sexes, each with a distinct aesthetic sense, might have resulted in a likable, diverse, and interesting people, if they weren't so aggressive and paranoid.

Try to avoid contact with any N'8ght at all.

N'8ght going a-courting

Tandu

Fierce and warlike, proto-Tandu were found by the N'8ght roughly 27 million years ago on a rocky and forbidding homeworld. Astonishingly, though proto-Tandu hives had barely any culture, they were already engaged in uplifting clients of their own—domesticated animals bred for various traits, including raw intelligence and psychic ability. The Uplift Institute regards this early, unsupervised start as one reason why these clients seem quite insane.

Tandu commander (Thennanin spy recording)

Like their N'8ght patrons, the Tandu have a predilection for violence. Since achieving adult status, they have happily taken part in all major Galactic purges.

BIOLOGY ⊸
PSYCHOLOGY

Tandu are six-legged, warm-blooded insectoids—though unlike insects, they possess a completely efficient respiratory and circulatory system, allowing them to stand, on average, 3 meters tall. Their coloring ranges from tan-gold with brown markings to blue-green with black markings. Their mantis-like bodies walk on the back four legs, using the front two as manipulators. Chitinous armor is tough but brittle. Extremities, including heads, have the ability to regenerate.

Each of six eye-pods holds a brain. These work in tandem, coming to a "consensus" on decisions or concepts. When an idea results in an especially bad outcome, the brain that originated it is nipped off and a new head-bud is grown, hopefully to think more productive thoughts. Like many Terran insects, Tandu communicate by racheting and rubbing body parts together.

Being sexless, they lack some of the joyful charms of their N'8ght patrons. Instead, Tandu are hermaphroditic, exchanging genes by eating the spore-pods of dead Tandu who won credit in campaigns against infidels.

Everybody is an infidel.

Tandu are extreme xenophobes, even toward their own patrons and clients, who are tolerated rather than liked. Around other species, Tandu often engage in nervous pacing and leg-scratching.

This is a case where Terragen agents should practice a little xenophobia of their own.

Tandu are among the last species to follow tenets of the Inheritor Alliance, a pseudo-religious philosophy based on belief that the Progenitors willed control of the Five Galaxies to their most closely related clients—those leading down to the N'8ght Clan. Inheritors see themselves as holy warriors, chosen to cleanse the universe of heretics—at which point the Progenitors will return to pass judgment on the Five Galaxies. Since all other clans are heretics, some say it is only a matter of time before they attempt a "cleansing." Only the essentially lawful nature of Galactic society, and the Tandu's fearsome reputation, has prevented other alliances from ganging together to make these terrifying creatures extinct.

Some worry that things could easily go the other way around.

SOCIETY ⚬ CONTACT WITH EARTHLINGS

Proto-Tandu were pack-hunting carnivores. To this day they prefer to dismember live game, and have been known to do this to members of sapient species, often condemned criminals that other clans trade to the Tandu in exchange for Aivvern spice or Gloor. Tandu almost always volunteer for war parties called up by the Galactic Institutes, to help chastise wayward races for violations of innumerable codes. Their overenthusiastic participation has at times contributed to the "unfortunate" extinction of several species.

Tandu have a regimented, hierarchical society. The Inheritor Alliance invests its priesthood with total life-and-death control. This follows in genetically manipulating their clients to blind, subservient roles. Acceptors and Episiarchs are considered mad by Galactic standards, incapable of surviving without Tandu guidance.

Ideally, you should not converse with a Tandu without witnesses—or at all. They sometimes bite impulsively, and justify it later. A Tymbrimi or Kanten companion can help reinforce your status as a patron-level sapient. A Thennanin can give even more clout. Tandu fear no other race, but they do respect the Thennanin, Soro, and other high-ranking warrior clans.

If contact with a Tandu seems inevitable without witnesses, your safest bet is to prepare a vodor programmed with a standard apology in Gal Eight, lay the vodor on the floor, set to replay, and exit as quickly as possible.

Acceptor

(ac-CEP-tor) a Acceptor /-ab Tandu -ab N'8ght

Acceptor (Thennanin spy recording)

The Tandu have closed all files concerning their clients, declaring religious privacy reasons. Fifty-seven clans and alliances have filed appeals with the Library Institute, protesting this flagrant abuse of privilege. A preliminary injunction against the Tandu is expected in less than a thousand years.

For the time being, there are no openly accessible Library entries on Acceptor biology. In fact, there have been few actual sightings of this unique species, though Intelligence reports that Tandu genetic manipulation accentuated their psychic abilities at the cost of other sapient traits, in violation of standard Uplift practice.

Acceptors are rumored to be 1.75 to 2 meters tall, quadruped, without tool manipulators (another Uplift violation). Their carapace is sectioned in three parts, like Terrestrial insects, with legs branching from the joints between body sections. A spiral sensing organ on the end of a proboscis may be scent-related.

One Thennanin noted that Acceptors move with a gangly, uneven gait, suggesting they are perpetually off balance, perhaps due to their skewed perception of reality. Acceptors may play a major role in

Episiarch and Acceptor
(Thennanin spy
recording)

the Tandu probability-based stardrive by taking in, psychically, all that is going on around them. They can read radiation from star systems as well as minds, making hardly any distinction between the two. It's all the same—random input—to an Acceptor.

Acceptors reportedly have no society of their own. It is unlikely you will ever see one, but organic samples of Acceptor tissue are on the list of Priority 2 Desiderata. If you gain access to a Tandu-owned Library branch, copy all files relating to their clients.

Episiarch

(e-PEES-iarch) a Episiarch /-ab Tandu -ab N'8ght

The Tandu have closed all files concerning these clients. This is under appeal. (See *Acceptor*.)

Sightings of Episiarchs are rare. They resemble white, shaggy bears, with almost featureless faces. We know the creatures are psi adepts of extraordinary force, whose talents appear rooted in a powerful, ego-driven rejection of reality as-is, provoking causality-probability fluctuations in their vicinity.

One Terragen agent recorded an encounter with an Episiarch under Tandu

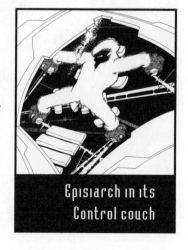

Episiarch in its
Control couch

control. The creature appeared to be materializing a space-time portal by psychic projection alone, enabling its master to escape an unpleasant social function.

On a larger scale, Episiarchs apparently play a role in the Probability Stardrive. Thennanin scholars suggest that the Tandu may even have attempted to jump an entire planet through N-space, using a cluster of Episiarchs, en masse. They doubt that the test succeeded.

Episiarchs reportedly are separated from their mothers before their eyes open, and thus they have no society other than serving the Tandu. When sighted, Episiarchs are often held in check with a harness, leash, or some kind of neural probe. After an Episiarch reaches maturity, it is kept much of the time in "chambers of delusion" to keep it distracted.

The only time you are likely to encounter an Episiarch is if you are being trailed by a Tandu hunting party. Try to survive, and report about the experience.

Incrementor

(in-cre-MEN-tor) a Incrementor /-ab Tandu -ab N'8ght

Incrementor and Episiarch
[Thennanin spy recording]

As with other Tandu clients, records about Incrementors are sealed. Probing through a Library branch on Tanith did uncover one piece of information—Incrementors were the first race the Tandu uplifted. Yet, in formal introductions they are listed last, suggesting a demotion in status.

Incrementors have been seen only twice, at a distance, by Terragen agents. They resemble multi-legged dandelions with sensory nodules circling below a globe of soft fuzz. Thennanin claim the Incrementors' tentacles have minute barbs along the entire length, for grasping and manipulation.

Incrementors are likely to be as insane as the rest of their clan.

They seem to be given a wide berth, even by other Tandu clients, and are sure to be psi-adepts. We don't know how they serve the Tandu, and that makes them especially frightening. If you encounter an Incrementor, with or without its patron, back away and try to observe quietly.

Looks Are Deceiving—
Star Clan of the Gubru

Ot'ahh

(OOT-ahhh) a Ot'ahh ∕ -ul Kooyio -ul Gooksyu -ul Gubru -ul Kwackoo -ul
Okukoo

Ot'ahh gaming

Extrapolating from their great-grandclients, the Gubru, Ot'ahh would have been rigid xeno-phobes. But they appear in Galactic records as one of the Six Hero Races that vanished with the Tarseuh after routing the "Lions." If you bump into one, it means the Six Hero Races are coming back and all hell is going to break loose. This would be almost as startling as the Progenitors showing up at your door to sell Amway products.

Kooyio

(KOO-eeoo) a Kooyio /-ab Ot'ahh /-ul Gooksyu -ul Gubru -ul Kwackoo -ul Okukoo

Granddaddies of the ornery Gubru, Kooyio distinguished themselves early as mediators with the Institute for Civilized Warfare. They are officially retired and in the beginning stages of "transcendence," yet a few have been spotted at rare Galactic social functions. If you are honored enough to be allowed near one, find a senior agent and follow all ceremonial procedures to the letter.

Kooyio engineer

Gooksyu

(GOOK-seeoo) a Gooksyu /-ab Kooyio -ab Ot'ahh /-ul Gubru -ul Kwackoo -ul Okukoo

The patrons of the Gubru were uplifted 27 million years ago, and at first seemed eager innovators at anything they could lay their feathered hands on. Though the Library Institute supposedly knows all, the Kooyio encouraged their clients to continue experimenting at most everything. We're not sure whether this trait was self-suppressed, as

Gooksyu ambassadors

the Gooksyu discovered that the Galactic Library contained more concepts than one race could ever conceive, or if they simply grew lazy or frustrated as more Galactic technology became available. Still, they support the Institute for Progress and voted in favor of Earth-inspired research projects... irritating their Gubru heirs.

These short bipedal avians resemble eyeless toucans with spindly legs. Gooksyu have a vision strip around their heads, without lenses to serve as focal mechanisms. Their coloring—bright, almost fluorescent—cues hormonal changes for mating, as in the Gubru. Likewise, the Gooksyu passed on their societal structure of suzerains.

While the Gooksyu are proud of their clan, and have been known for fierceness in times past, the Gubru have taken ever greater control, pushing the Gooksyu into a somewhat resentful semiretirement.

Gooksyu only appear at functions with heavily armed guards. This seems to be more the idea of the Gubru than their esteemed patrons.

Gubru

(GOO-broo) a Gubru /-ab Gooksyu -ab Kooyio -ab Ot'ahh /-ul Kwackoo -ul Okukoo

---

Gubru are a wealthy and ambitious race, uplifted by the Gooksyu 1.5 million years ago from a single "flock" inhabiting the major continent on their homeworld. Similar avian species on other continents proved profoundly resistant to gene manipulation, resulting in parallel evolutionary paths, like the great apes and humans on Earth. As flightless avian life-forms, average adult Gubru resemble gangly birds, approximately 1.8 meters tall, but weighing only 30 kilograms. They stand, ostrich-like, on three-toed legs. The stork-like beak has an extensible tongue, which may play a part in the sexual triad of mating.

Gubru are very fast and their legs can be deadly in close combat. Their arms are relatively weak, and the Gubru are not adept at heavy manual labor.

All Gubru start life as white-feathered neuters. A few lucky ones are selected by special committees to be given a liqueur that triggers development of both sexuality and gentry plumage. This plumage evokes obedience from lesser Gubru. The elect are chosen in groups of three, whenever some project, enterprise, or expedition requires leaders in command. Members of the trio both collaborate and compete with each other in a complex system that eventually results in a dominant individual becoming a red-feathered queen. The remaining two transform into blue- or amber-colored males. The dynamics of the triad never actually stabilize, but a "pecking order" emerges, determining how much influence each has on the others, and the enterprise over which they are jointly ruling.

Both males are necessary for the triad to produce a multi-egg clutch.

(ALERT: Do not be fooled by superficial similarities to Earthly birds. Gubru remain organically alien beings!)

SOCIETY ○ CONTACT WITH EARTHLINGS

Gubru have a strange way of mixing sex and politics. The mating ritual intertwines with the managing of the most mundane facets of Gubru life. Three seats of power in any major enterprise are occupied by *suzerains,* representing priestly, commercial, and military castes. Though intelligent and capable of skilled work, the average neuter Gubru has low self-motivation. They make good, obedient technicians and soldiers. Mid-level bureaucrats have a bit more initiative, but are subject to the will of their suzerains. Sexually active Gubru, on the other hand, are capable of both shrewdness and decisive action, though important decisions call for consensus with their mates. High-echelon princes and queens are constantly alert for opportunities to advance the wealth and dominance of their clan.

Gubru appear to be humorless and conservative. They are not religious fanatics, like the Jophur and Tandu. But a prudish insistence on tradition and protocol often amounts to the same thing. They speak Gal Three on formal occasions, employ more rapid Gal Four in everyday situations, and use vodors for speech with non-clan races.

Because of our "wolfling" status, Gubru are contemptuous of Terragens, an attitude inflamed by recent developments at our colony on Garth. However, because of Gooksyu breeding, they are strictly bound by Galactic rules. This can sometimes work to our advantage.

If in a negotiating situation, follow Galactic protocols scrupulously. This can put the punctilious Gubru in a position where they cannot avoid treating Earthlings decently.

It is doubtful that a Gubru would let itself be in close proximity to any Terragen agent without being armed. You should be discreetly prepared.

Gubru Suzerains

Kwackoo

(KWA-coo) a Kwackoo /-ab Gubru -ab Gooksyu -ab Kooyio -ab Ot'ahh

The Gubru, in their xenophobia, rejected several Uplift candidates in order to seek bird-like clients. Proto-Kwackoo (not their original name) used to hunt all across their native world in flocks of pterodactyl-like predators, using primitive nets to attack and consume all sorts of land and sea beasts, driving many to the verge of extinction. The Gubru were impressed, and quickly negotiated a contract to adopt them.

Over 2 meters tall when sitting up, Kwackoo are now four-footed and landbound. The front hands bend out of the way when walking. An extra knee/elbow facilitates grasping and feeding. Rear legs have a bony extension, letting them balance on four points when sitting. The breastplate of a Kwackoo extends over half a meter from its lower thorax, covering the mouth and breathing nostrils.

The head is a Kwackoo's most unusual feature, incredibly streamlined with no surface breaks. The top ridge shelters a hearing organ. On either side are triangular fins, mounted on muscular stalks. These contain optical sensors. Like their masters, the Kwackoo speak Gal Three and Four, but because of their large vocal cavity, they speak two octaves lower than the Gubru.

Since they are only 20,000 years into their indenture, Kwackoo are eager students of the Gubru. Their background as cooperative pack/swarm hunters contributes to a cheerful team-oriented mentality, approaching the most menial task with polite enthusiasm. Kwackoo have been promised that their society will be given room to evolve on its own, after proper indoctrination.

Under most circumstances Kwackoo show complete loyalty to the Gubru. But since Gubru suzerains are often fiercely competitive, their clients, too, often are at odds with each other. Terragen agents have at times been able to do favors and establish mutually beneficial relationships with individual Kwackoo. Exercise caution.

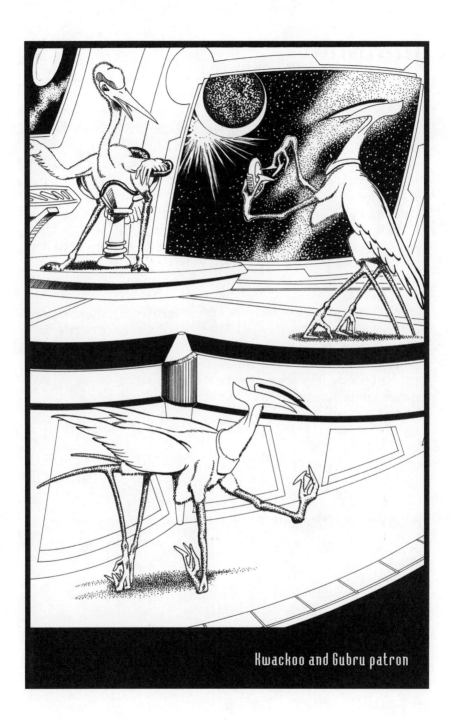

Kwackoo and Gubru patron

Okukoo

Gubru discovered the Okukoo on a bright, light, pampas-covered planet. After 35,000 years, they are less than halfway through their indenture. On their homeworld, flocks of millions of these leaf-eaters blotted out the sun when passing overhead, yet Okukoo would never completely defoliate an area, as some might expect. Subconsciously, they seemed to understand a need for sustainability, making them candidates for Uplift, despite a lack of any tool-using skills.

The first humans to see an Okukoo likened it to a "vertical hummingbird" with four wings equilaterally set around the torso. Ten dark eyes are spaced below a four-jawed beak. Tentacles hang below the torso for manipulation. They are known to lift several times their own weight.

Like their co-clients, the Kwackoo, they seem eager and polite. And like their Gubru patrons, they lack any trace of a sense of humor. With Uplift-augmented intelligence, they are being modified for service as highly agile messengers and engineers. It is hard to get to know an Okukoo, because they seldom hover in one place long enough to start a conversation. No human has ever seen an Okukoo set down.

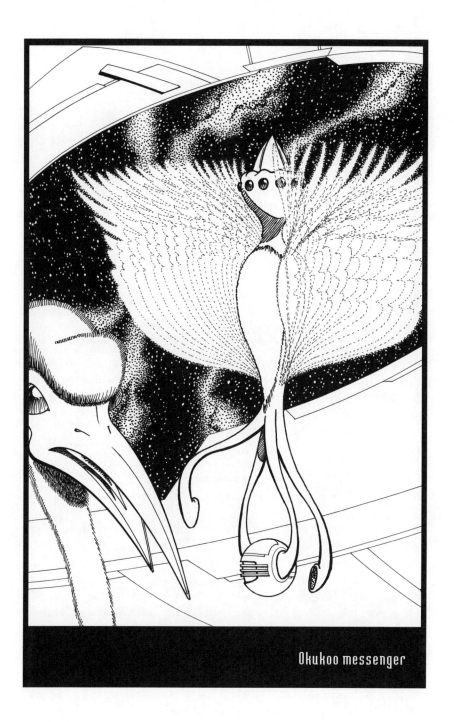

Okukoo messenger

More Enigmas—
Komahd Clan

Komahd

(ko-MAED) a Komahd /-ab Tumahd /-ul Mn'n

NOTE TO JUNIOR AGENTS: It is not uncommon for patrons to name a client species after some desirable attribute. For example "Paha" means "loyal" in Gal Six, a bit like naming your dog "Fido." There are no less than three Main Sequence species called "Paha" in the Five Galaxies at this time.

Thus, the species covered in this section is not to be confused with a minor insectoid client of the Soro—a-Komahd ab-Gello. The similarity ends with their names.

In Gal Eight, "Komahd" stands for "relentless."

Komahd pre-sentients were fierce amphibious carnivores. While uplifting them, their Tumahd patrons had to enforce a strict police state to keep the Komahd from slaughtering each other. In spite of this, they fulfilled all requirements for Galactic citizenship . . . with the Tumahd pulling a few strings. Komahd life is very structured so that each individual may control his/her fierce impulses by following strict, memorized procedures.

Komahd do not like surprise.

BIOLOGY ◦ PSYCHOLOGY

Tripodal centaurs, they have an alligator-like appearance. Their arms have two elbow joints each. Long fingers appear light and delicate, but are able to crush shelled mollusks on their homeworld. Their

Komahd religious cultist

most notable feature is a multi-hinged mouth, letting them open to almost ninety degrees. A large, pelican-like pouch allows ingestion of sizable food items, generally still living.

Two of the three legs were originally fins, giving Komahdi the look of a centaur grafted onto a manta ray. Obviously, their evolutionary path was a complex one. They still spend a lot of time in water. Submerged, the rear leg flattens, with webbing, to become a powerful tail-propulsor. While Komahd industry takes place on land, much of their civilization and home life occurs underwater, so it's been hard to learn much about them. We hope to correct this when Dolphin agents (disguised as merchants and tourists) infiltrate cosmopolitan planets Zuma and Riecher.

Their homeworld was a fierce one and Komahd ancestors often had to flee into the surf from land predators, then dash ashore from those hunting them at sea. They weren't highest on their home evolutionary food chain, and still react with suspicion at a primal level. It is best not to use irony or sarcasm with these creatures. They will simply assume it means you are a liar.

Mn˙n

(MN-enn) a Mn'n /-ab Komahd -ab Tumahd

The Komahd found the Mn'n a willing, eager client race. Keen on achieving status in Galactic society, the Mn'n asked that the Komahd perform gene-engineering as radical as possible without provoking the wrath of the Institute for Uplift. They rapidly passed all required tests, evidently hoping for early graduation to adult-patron status—only to face obstinate refusal from the Tumahd. Mn'n face many more millennia of servitude before being allowed the status they feel they deserve.

According to the Galactic Library, Mn'n are oviparous parasites. They coexist with a pint-sized animal, the *sulm,* which goes through metamorphosis in a self-made cocoon to evolve from adolescent to adult form. A female Mn'n uses her ovipositor to place one egg in a coccooned sulm. In prehistory, this may have been purely predatory, but today a symbiosis exists. The Mn'n parent provides nutrients, enabling both the sulm and the hatchling Mn'n to survive, most of the time. In fact, Mn'n breed favorite sulm broodlines and even talk of someday uplifting the species, creating a truly equal partnership.

This plan ran into an obstacle, however. The Komahd have in-

Mn'n engineers

fected the sulm with half of a binary virus. Neither half is toxic by itself, but the combined effect is lethal. Should the Mn'n ever get uppity, the Komahd can eliminate most of their sulm breeding stock. This fiendish scheme evades the rules against threatening an intelligent species with genocide *directly.* So for now the Mn'n seem trapped.

Mn'n seem capable of farsightedness and compassion, perhaps rooted in their complex view of sexuality (involving not only two sexes but also two species). And yet, their deep origins as a predatory parasite come through at other times, hinting at sudden ruthlessness. It is an eerie combination.

A theorist in the Terragen Uplift Center suggests that if we (or any other sapient race) could offer the Mn'n genetic cures for the sulm, they would eagerly desert their patrons. Such a program would be a lengthy task, requiring concealment from Tumahd Clan. For obvious reasons, we are not ready to take on such a dangerous and subtle game of Galactic intrigue.

Can Sour Turn Sweet?—

Star Clan of the Hoon and Guthatsa

Guthatsa

(Gu-THAT-sah) a Guthatsa /-ul Hoon

Five hundred and twenty-three thousand years ago, the proto-Guthatsa were four-legged herbivores. Even after Uplift straightened their posture, the Guthatsa only average 1.5 meters tall. Their skin is a fine-grain leather with a greenish gray tone. The dust gills below their eyeflaps are usually a bright red. Feeding cilia are gold to lime green. Short cilia on either side of their head filter grains off wheat-like stalks. Even more obsessive than their Hoon clients, the Guthatsa have become vital "bean counters" in Galactic society. Many Guthatsa are senior members of the Institute for Navigation and Trade, and the Institute for Foresight.

Hoon

(HOOOON) a Hoon /-ab Guthatsa

The Guthatsa discovered the proto-Hoon 287,000 years ago, fascinated by the creatures' haunting musical voices, booming across the mountain vales of their nursery world. Beyond giving their new clients all of the normal gifts—such as speech, reasoning, and other traits nec-

Guthatsa "bean counter"

essary for Galactic intercourse—the Guthatsa also enhanced the vibrant output of the Hoonish throat sac.

Hoon have been minor players in Galactic affairs, providing countless dour, bureaucratic functionaries to the various Institutes. They also serve as the strong-arm of the Guthatsa, when called upon.

BIOLOGY

Hoon are bipedal, reaching up to 2.5 meters tall, with two elbow joints per arm, and two knee joints per leg. A Hoon's body is covered in leathery scales, except where the forearms and forelegs bear mats of coarse hair. Their spinal cord is encased in a structure that does not completely grow as they mature. At puberty, a Hoon sheds its youthful spine for a stronger adult replacement, dropping the old one in chunks. A flood of hormones then pushes the Hoon body to maturity in months.

Hoon are intensely proud of two physical features—their noses and the resonant voices that first drew attention their way. (Compliments are welcome and flattery can prove effective.) The throat sac on an adult male Hoon, when fully inflated, is over half a meter wide. It emits multilevel chords, sounding like a cross between a foghorn and a cello. But an angry Hoon may screech like an amplified bagpipe. The "umble" is a counterpoint behind most Hoon speech, denoting both mood and underlying meanings.

In Galactic terms, the Hoon are listed as "low breeders," devoting great attention to one offspring at a time.

PSYCHOLOGY

Most Hoon we have encountered are stodgy pencil-pushers, having a tendency to get bogged down in details of any situation. As officious bureaucrats, they are often the first to say that something can't be done, because the Library says it's never been tried. These officials exhibit annoyance at Earthlings when we persist.

Within their own clan, the Hoon are protective and familial. Indeed, an obvious devotion to their children is seen as their most endearing trait. Some have been observed showing kindness toward the youth of other species, though they grow cold toward adults.

Unfortunately, their involvement in the suppression of the Terragen colony at NuDawn has left a sour taste between Hoons and Earthclan. Ironically, they seem even more bitter over having been "forced" to act cruelly than we are over seeing one of our colonies savagely put down.

Clearly, something is going on, deep inside the Hoon. They act very unhappy. Some human psychologists claim to see evidence of a re-

Hoon customs officials

pressed racial personality, just waiting to break out. Others warn that it is just crazy to view an alien race in our own terms.

SOCIETY ⇔ CONTACT WITH EARTHLINGS

Hoon sometimes attempt to follow their patrons' lead as aggressive Galactic politicians, but they can be foiled in the details. Intentional glitches in information can stop a Hoon dead cold, offering a good stalling tactic while they try to sort things out. Do not use this ploy too frequently, though. Hoon react badly if they think they are being deliberately lied to.

Just Plain Weird, but Don't Say That to Their "Face" —
Clan of T'4Lek

Saovimvah

(sa-o-VIM-va) a Saovimvah / -ul Poaglisis -ul T'4Lek -ul L'92Thit -ul K'8Fu -ul J'9Tisiss -ul Voag'8M

The Saovimvah were among the originators of the Institute for Civilized Warfare, but now seem to be in the last stages of retirement, hoping to transcend to the next level and join the Progenitors. Four meters tall, Saovimvah are said to share Retirement worlds with their clients, the Poaglisis. The two races may have decided to achieve transcendence together, not as patron and client, but as partners. On rare occasions, they invite younger races to send emissaries to philosophical conclaves, held deep in the gravity wells of a "fractal" retirement world. Luckily, the Terragen Council was invited to the next one, in just 312 years... assuming we survive that long. A great honor, bypassing many more senior races, the invitation added to both our prestige and the resentment that some hold toward us.

Agents are encouraged, if possible, to seek clues as to *why* we were so honored. One possible hint—the Saovimvah also requested that Earth send along a humpback whale.

Saovimvah

Poaglisis

(Po-AG-LEES-is) a Poaglisis /-ab Saovimvah /-ul T'4Lek -ul L'92Thit -ul K'8Fu -ul J'9Tisiss -ul Voag'8M

Poaglisis were uplifted by the great Soavimvah 1.6 million years ago. They are huge quadrupeds, averaging 2 meters tall, with tree-stump-like legs. The "mushroom" on top is a saucer-shaped head with dozens of small eyes. Body coloring is a beautiful azure blue, while the head is a flaming Chinese red. Though uplifted by one of the most tolerant races in the Five Galaxies, Poaglisis need the sapients they encounter to be clothed for religious reasons. This distances them from several clans that see body coverings as a distracting annoyance.

Past Terragen agents have only encountered the Poaglisis at formal gatherings but haven't had the opportunity to observe them in daily Galactic life. The Earth branch Library has little information on them.

T'4Lek

(tee-GLOTTAL CLICK-Leck) a T'4Lek /-ab Poaglisis -ab Saovimvah /-ul L'92Thit -ul K'8Fu -ul J'9Tisiss -ul Voag'8M

T'4Lek history is longer than the Soro's, having been uplifted 470 million years ago by the Poaglisis. The giant arches were found on their homeworld thundering across vast plains of prairie grass. One interesting note: It seems that it took the Poaglisis several centuries just to convince the T'4Lek that a Galactic society existed at all. Since then, they have devoted most of their external activities to the Great Library, notably in the History Department as *watchers,* documenting events.

T'4Lek are 3-meter-tall mobile archways. A row of optical sensors runs along each side of the upper arch. The inner edge next to the ground level has a row of ⅓-meter-long cilia. The ribbed area on the underside of the arch appears to be a series of lungs. Biologically, they seem related to lichen, possibly as two or three organisms in symbiosis. T'4Lek are saprophytic, obtaining nutrients from nonliving organic matter. Reproduction is by division. Movement occurs via a rippling motion

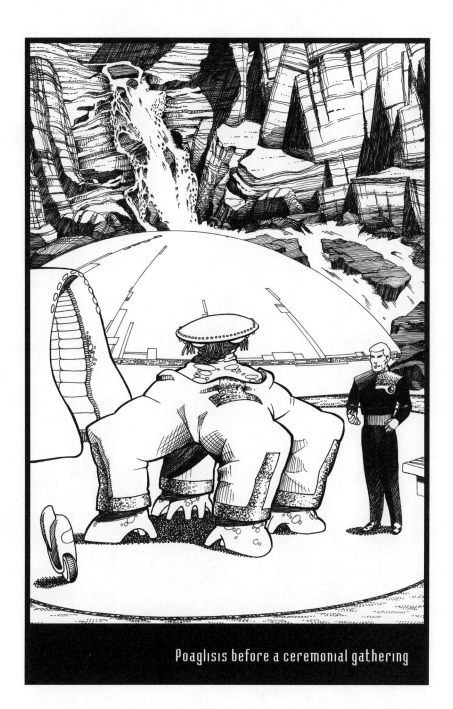

Poaglisis before a ceremonial gathering

along each arch base. Thennanin records show a T'4Lek "running," leaping from base to base, using them like legs. The average life span of a T'4Lek is over 1,000 years.

As multiple-personalities, T'4Lek are probably some of the more stable entities in Galactic society. They have a great sense of honor and history, yet in conversation they are brutally honest about the realities of Galactic events. Even with their honesty, they do not want active involvement in most Galactic affairs.

Saovimvah and T'4Lek

Stranger Still—

The Xatınnı

Xatınnı

(Za-TEE-nee) a Xatinni /-ab Xaal /-ul Xap

Xatinni were uplifted 4.2 million years ago by the Xaal. They shaved almost a third of the standard 100,000 years off their indenture. Chimp-like in posture, Xatinni are shorter than humans. The head is bent back on the neck, spreading out like a reverse hammerhead. A black and tan ring-like pattern to their fur gives the Xatinni an ocelot appearance.

Xatinni are solitary beings. According to the Galactic Library, individuals store genetic material on graduating from "commerce school," then head out to do business with the rest of Galactic society, leaving reproduction to artificial incubation centers. They are rarely seen in pairs.

Negotiating is a big deal to Xatinni, who are offended if you pay the first price mentioned. Tymbrimi tell of a ship purchase

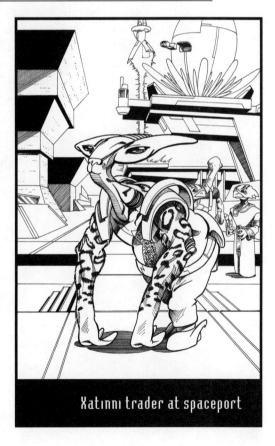

Xatınnı trader at spaceport

from Xatinni traders taking a decade to complete. One wonders why they bother.

Xap

(ZAP) a Xap /-ab Xatinni -ab Xaal

The sole client of the Xatinni, Xap were uplifted 1.3 million years ago. The odd thing about the proto-Xap homeworld was its lack of animal life. We suspect that the Xap ravaged all other mobile species to extinction. When pressed, the Xatinni admit that proto-Xap were heading into cannibalism when Uplift rescued them. The Institute for Migration also notes the Xap have been cited several times for ecosystem abuse.

Xap have radial symmetry, with four arms and four legs arranged evenly around a central vertical axis. An array of optical fibers fan out above the shoulders. The "hands" are bundles of six to eight tentacles blending with the long fur of the flexible arms.

Xap mate and travel for life in pairs. From short encounters at public functions, they appear to feel they are neurotic underlings of a minor patron—an accurate assessment.

Xap are constantly looking for a profit, perhaps because of pressures put on them by the Xatinni. Approach business dealings with them by preplanning favors and responses for the next several years. Like their patrons, the Xap have occasionally stumbled across valuable information and are willing to sell.

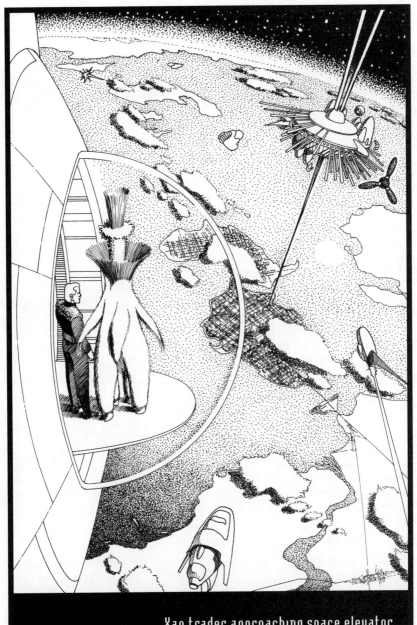

Xap trader approaching space elevator

Lost Wonders—
The G'Kek

Drooli

(DRU-lee) a Drooli / -ul G'Kek

On their homeworld proto-Drooli were, believe it or not, tree-dwelling. Their soon-to-be patrons found these arboreal slugs draped, wide and flat, across the tops of vast bulacacia trees, slowly munching on leaves and soaking up rays. Surprisingly for such sedentary life-forms, they were pre-sapient and ready for adoption. Uplift was smooth for the huge mollusks, who had the good fortune of entering Galactic society between major upheavals, at a time of exceptional tolerance.

Drooli resemble giant sea slugs with manipulative tentacles along two main ridges on their backs. Some ridges form linear "eyes" like an insect's. Movement is snail-like, with a rippling motion of their foot muscle. Coloring is generally a shale gray, though they have been seen to change color like a squid or octopus.

Drooli have had to cope with enmity from several extremist clans, for reasons we still are trying to understand. Their clients, the equally bizarre G'Kek, were apparently wiped out because of a grudge held by the Obeyor Alliance.

Drooli researcher on Institute grounds

G'Kek

(g-KEKK) a G'kek /-ab Drooli

HISTORY

Although this is a minor race—and probably extinct—we include it as a cautionary tale about how dangerous the universe can be.

Drooli explorers found the proto-G'Kek already close to sapience, living quietly in an obscure planetary system that the Library had listed as "unlikely" to produce any adoptable species. In fact, strong evidence suggests that these creatures were the devolved remnants of a sapient race that retired from the Galactic scene millions of years before. Having reshaped themselves physically, then restored their innocence through a process called "redemption," they were ready to begin the adventure again, sponsored by a new patron.

Things began well for the renewed G'Kek. But unfortunately, Drooli Clan ran afoul of the Obeyor Alliance ten thousand years ago in a quasi-war of exceptional bitterness. The insouciant G'Kek became particular objects of hysterical Obeyor hatred, especially the Jophur, who launched a war of extermination.

Apparently they were successful. There have been no sightings of G'Kek for 2,000 years.

BIOLOGY ○ PSYCHOLOGY

A rarity in evolution, the G'Kek were a *wheeled* race. The wheels began as seven thin balloon-like bladders on motile stalks. Evolution— or perhaps genetic intervention by unknown forces—eventually fused the segments into a rigid rim. The hubs, mounted on independent axles, contained fibrous metal organs, which interacted with natural magnets in the torso to create an organic motor. Two hind legs, almost atrophied, provided additional traction by pushing. Young G'Kek were able to run on these legs till their wheel rims fused.

G'Kek had a vertical body with an L-shaped balancing tail-stalk. Two tentacled arms with three boneless fingers extended from a shoulderless torso. Adding to the eerie contours of this unusual being were four flexible vision-stalks, each with a single eye, surrounding a central vocal orifice. Anywhere from one to four eyes would focus on a scene, depending on how interesting it seemed.

Individuals were born with both male and female reproductive organs and consciously chose which sex to emphasize during puberty. During mating, a couple intertwined wheels while rolling back and

Still from G'Kek cable-riding competition

forth. The final act followed complex wheeled dances, often as part of a cable-riding ritual.

Somewhat heedless of personal safety, G'Kek appear to have been reckless gamblers. In fact, they lost their homeworld on a wager.

SOCIETY ◦ CONTACT WITH EARTHLINGS

After Uplift, nearly all G'Kek forsook planet-dwelling to go live on orbiting habitats. These space-faring web-hives consisted of vast, rotating cylindrical structures cross-connected by a myriad of thin cables that let these wheeled beings come into their own, zooming and swooping from place to place with an abandon that would never be possible on a gritty, natural world. Cable-riding competitions were frequent, resulting in many fatalities, yet the tradition only strengthened over time, reinforcing a daredevil reputation.

G'Keks are thought to be extinct, but there have been hints that some orbital habitats eluded the Obeyor vendetta, escaping into the vastnesses between the stars. If you chance on any further information about this, do follow up on it, at Priority Level Three. As fellow victims of fanatical forces, any surviving G'Kek may be valuable allies, or at least have insights to offer. If they truly have found the knack of hiding successfully from Galactic society, it is a secret we may have to use ourselves someday, if luck turns against the peoples of Earth.

Some Species Never Learn...
Bururalli

Bururalli

(Bur-ur-ALLEE) asu Bururalli /-ab Nahalli

Raised up by the Nahalli just 122,000 years ago, the Bururalli cut a swath through the ecologies of half a hundred worlds. Having barely passed certification as full Galactic citizens, they were trouble from the outset, swiftly abandoning or defying all of the planet-care rules that Galactic Institutes had developed across 3 billion years.

They quickly were made extinct.

Bururalli

Nahalli

(Na-HALL-ee) a Nahalli /-ulsu Bururalli /-ab Thennanin

Nahalli were uplifted 14.6 million years ago, but they apparently never took Galactic society seriously, considering its most hallowed rules to be mere suggestions. After the Bururalli Holocaust, 50,000 years ago, the Nahalli were heavily fined and dropped back to client status (under Thennanin guidance) for failing to prevent the tragedy. Though they hope to pay penance and return into proper society, some believe the Nahalli will never be allowed to uplift clients again.

Nahalli in navigation chair

Individual Starfaring Races

The following species are among those for which we have drastically incomplete histories or about which the Council wants to know more. We provide this partial list to encourage investigation by all Terragen agents in hope of finding new allies or new insights into Galactic society.

Glavers

(GLAV-ers) a Glaver /-ab Tunnuctyur /-ul Sumubulum

Glavers, a relatively minor citizen race, are best known as intermediaries and negotiators between the oxygen-breathing Civilization of Five Galaxies and various (mostly mysterious) hydrogen-breathing races that share much of known space. Despite this useful service, they have apparently been waning for about 10,000 years, having sold off all their planet-based holdings to live in mobile space structures. In fact, none of our contacts can report having seen one in about 2,000 years. The Tymbrimi find this fact "worrisome"—though sometimes races do vanish from sight for a while, only to show up again, setting up for business in another spiral arm.

These absences—"sabbaticals"—are a matter of some interest to the Terragen

Old still recording of Glavers trader

Council. Find out what you can about them, especially how such races manage to stay invisible for extended periods.

Glavers are reptilian in appearance. Their bulbous eyes are independent of each other, and swivel in a way disconcerting to most binocular races. Glavers are primarily quadrupedal, and use their prehensile forked tail in concert with their hands for gripping and manipulation.

Sumubulum

(sumeoo-beoo-LUM) a Sumubulum /-absu Glavers -ab Tunnuctyur

Proto-Sumubulum were found 113 million years ago by the Glavers on a large, rocky world orbiting a chain of small, brown dwarf suns. Their homeworld was not only wracked by wild perturbations from an irregular orbit, it was highly ovoid. Life had retreated to a few algae pools smaller than the Great Lakes on Earth. Since the Ch'th'turn Epoch, all Sumubulum have been seen in a variety of anti-G encounter suits, suggesting that they may have drifted quite far from the body plan shown in obsolete library records. They may be making drastic self-alterations in preparation for a coming time of chaos and change.

Ever since their patrons, the Glavers, dropped from sight, the Sumubulum have retired from all major Institutes, becoming more enigmatic, living on a series of Coal Sack worlds. They earn a living by offering translation and mediation services between oxygen-breathing and hydrogen-breathing races, arranging trades and short-term business deals with a minimum of fuss. They speak through their anti-G suits' vodors in a completely gender-neutral version of Gal Six.

At times, Sumubulum have purchased items from Terran sources that others thought useless, at high prices we barely comprehend. While these events were beneficial, they provoke questions. In this universe, anything mysterious can turn out to be dangerous.

Sumubulum in encounter suit

Karrank%

(kar-RANK-*glottal-stop*) a Karrank% /-ab Nr~klat -ab *Yrstk* -ab Slen

Here's another tragic cautionary tale, about a species called the Karrank%. Their patrons, the Nr~klat, were extremely hard on the proto-Karrank% during clienthood, making profound force-gene transformations and pushing the young race much faster than they were prepared for. Some of the imposed organic alterations seem bizarre and cruel. From a simple race of subterranean burrowers, digging tunnels and foraging under the roots of giant trees, they were turned into giant excavators who could delve into deep, hot layers of a planet's crust, seeking riches for their masters. The resulting pressures—both physical and mental—pushed the poor Karrank% past a breaking point. As emerging psi-adepts, they waited till a grand conclave of the Nr~klat was held, then mentally blasted their patrons back to a pre-sapient state.

The Uplift Institute thereupon resettled the traumatized Karrank% on isolated planet Kithrup—more of a recuperation than retirement. The 7-meter-tall Karrank% generally rest catatonically still, in vertical shafts, with the metal-tainted ocean damping much resentful force out of the psi-casts of their compatriots. No one knows if the abused creatures will ever climb back out of their deep holes in that distant world.

Karrank% have no known society, though Institute researchers have traced psi-cast dialogues between disparate Karrank% on remote areas of Kithrup. The "conversations" appeared to ramble without subject or time frame and last anywhere from seconds to weeks. Karrank% do not leave Kithrup and there are no plans by any Institute to push their recovery for the next half million years or so. Any interaction you might have with them would be on Kithrup—probably in a high-stress situation for both of you.

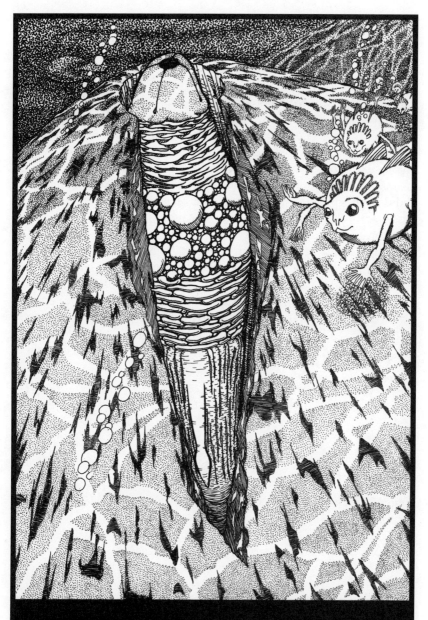

Karrank% mound opened for inspection by Institute

Mayha

(MEY-ha) a Mayha / -ab Chchhckt -ab Waoool -ab qob / -ul Squle -ul Fl'isl -ul Glnuph

Proto-Mayha were arboreal. As 2.25-meter-tall tripods, the Mayha have four arms—two for heavy lifting, anchored to big shoulder muscles ending with three massive "thumbers," and two inner manipulating arms with paired fingers and opposable thumbs. Bird-like eyes sit on opposite sides of a tall, smokestack-shaped head.

Mayha were among the few oxygen-breathing clans to befriend and defend so-called "rogue" machine races from discrimination and repression. This is consistent, since Mayha are inclined to augment themselves with artificial implants and processors. Sometimes the mass of machinery exceeds organic substance. This draws suspicion from some conservative alliances. Disclosure suits have been filed against them through the Institutes of Foresight and Civilized Warfare.

Contacts with human emissaries have been cautious but cordial, with certain Mahya expressing interest in our "wolfling" computer technologies. The matter is extremely delicate and junior agents must not get involved. Direct any inquiries to your superiors and document all contact.

Pargi

(PAR-gee) a Pargi / -ab Prochna -ab Hrnychi / -ul Brmoprm -ul Bl @ mtsht -ul Ixngi

Hexapodal centaurs, proto-Pargi were first discovered 111 million years ago on a cold planet in a Mars-like orbit plowing through a dust cloud. There is evidence that they did not originate on the world where they were found. Two hypotheses are either that they moved on their own and later devolved or else a patron race seeded them there for protection and eventual Uplift. If they moved on their own, the Pargi may be the oldest living "wolfling" race. Nevertheless, despite their lack of an ancient lineage Pargi have become influential, especially in weaving relationships among the countless "lesser" clans.

The average Pargi stands just under 2 meters tall. Heavy brows cover oversized—but very human—eyes. Horns branch out from ridges

Augmented Mayha

behind the eyebrows, spiraling toward each other. These are generally decorated with jewels and other ornamentation. The upper torso sits more in the middle of the lower torso than one might expect. Their four-jointed arms have a dexterity not seen in most creatures with a skeleton. Pargi skin is soft like suede.

Pargi have been known to welcome Terran observers to clan meetings and festivities, and reciprocated by expressing interest in Celtic and Druid rituals, which seem to have parallels in pre-Uplift Pargi society. More important, the Pargi have lately made known their displeasure over the way some sociopolitical and religious fanatic groups are throwing their weight around. They find especially irksome Soro and Tandu meddling in the flow of information across the Five Galaxies.

Pargi are currently among the leaders of a newly re-formed League of Prudent Neutral Clans, a loose and cautious—but numerically significant—organization. With luck, the Pargi have the potential to lead a fresh force for tolerance in a new Galactic order.

From this description, one may expect friendship from the Pargi, but any help could be a long time coming. "Moderates" move slowly in Galactic society. And they are, after all, aliens.

> **NOTE TO AGENTS: See if you can forge personal relationships with individual Pargi you meet, but refer any diplomatic contacts to higher levels.**

Paha

(pa-HA) a Paha / -ab Sniktt

Not to be confused with the minor client species Paha ab-Soro, which is covered in your normal class curriculum. The Paha discussed here are much more formidable. The Sniktt found proto-Paha decimating their arid homeworld in a pre-sapient war that had lasted over 20,000 years. Paha leaders readily accepted Uplift as a way to stop this conflict and focus on bigger foes.

Burly, 1.8-meter-tall bipedal reptiloids, adult Paha mass over 200 kilos and resemble huge Sumo wrestlers, or giant shell-less terrapins. Nostrils sit high above the mouth on a face that seems in a permanent scowl, even when they are supposedly in good humor.

Watch out for the pointed claws. Paha body chemistry is toxic to Terragens.

Pargi Neutral Clan representative

Paha are the police arm of the small but fierce Sniktt Clan. They would be considered thugs in a human culture, if they weren't so polite while going about their work. They have filed several petitions with the Uplift Institute, requesting patronage of newly found pre-sapients. Evidence points to the Sniktt squelching all of these, for unknown reasons.

NOTE: The Thennanin report skirmishes with regiments of Paha working for the Soro, and suspect they are mercenaries, leased by the Sniktt. We would like to know how the Paha feel about dying in large numbers for this arrangement.

Paha tech with bots in access shafts

Qheuen

(zuew-U-en) a Qheuen /-ab Zhosh

The pragmatic Zhosh, in uplifting these crab-like creatures, left the Qheuen's pre-sapient power structure in place, with gray-carapaced matriarchs dominating the other two classes—blues and reds—in hive-societies that were far looser than an ant colony, but more rigid than a feudal kingdom. Proto-Qheuen were a warring race, with constant clashes between hives. Today's uplifted versions have competitive rivalries that seem less violent but more relentless.

Ranging from 1.5 to 3 meters in diameter, these armored pentapods have no distinct front or back. Their "head" is a cupola that rises from the center of their body, then drops to protect the ribbon-like eye that wraps around a cylindrical brain-case. The legs are jointed like a lobster's, with a manipulative claw on each tip. There are five voice-boxes, one between each leg-joint to the main body.

Grays are proud of their position atop the race hierarchy and symbolize this by setting up homes on rocky heights. Red Qheuen prefer life in ocean shallows and display an innate curiosity about everything. Blues, by Galactic standards, seem to be the most "grounded." Their homes tend to be in or near freshwater lakes. It is curious that these three branches lived in such different environments, yet remained bound together in an ancient dominance structure. Perhaps the Zhosh enhanced Gray control as a means of ensuring their own.

Qheuen

Like their patrons, the Zhosh, the Qheuen are a minor race at the moment. While contact and diplomacy should be maintained with this group, for now they have little influence or power.

Rothen

(ROW-then) a Rothen / -ab?

Rothen have mysteriously appeared near Terragen-settled areas in the last century or so. No one has been able to determine where they make their home, though we are investigating leads to several planet-oidal "outposts." The Migration Institute lists Rothen as "itinerant," along with several dozen other races that have no fixed base or lease-hold. Their sparse Library entry shows lineage predating almost every existing race in known space, but this information is almost univer-sally discredited as a ruse, implanted during the last wave of data plagues. Rothen go on to profess that they subtly influence almost every sociopolitical arena, while keeping themselves aloof from the normal bustle of Galactic life.

In fact, many clans simply avoid all contact with them. Others are known to employ Rothen as mercenary spies, agents, or enforcers, since they do seem to have a knack for slipping in and out of sight, forging identities and vanishing from the Galactic scene whenever a situation seems too hot. They are Galactic citizens and pay minimum Institute dues, but even Tymbrimi and Thennanin scholars have little to say about these elusive beings. Some believe even the name "Rothen" is a ruse, used by numerous different quasi-criminal enter-prises over the years.

And yet, they appear to be a handsome and elegant people, with strikingly humanoid proportions. Five-fingered hands, long and lithe, are laid out like ours. Indeed, the similarities seem too pretty to be true. Library depictions of their graceful features show signs of tamper-ing, perhaps from intentional infection with data-corrupting viruses. Ironically, this interference seems only to have helped the Rothen, en-hancing their reputation as skilled behind-the-scenes meddlers for hire.

RECENT NOTE: There have been several sightings of an-other, unrecorded species fitting the basic proportions of Rothen. The face of this creature is chinless and spiny, with pronounced bony cranial ridges. (See accompanying enlargement of a photo taken at a Thennanin commer-cial outpost.) Rothen are known to have bio-sculpted changes in their appearance many times in the past. So this may be a separate subbranch, left over from earlier times.

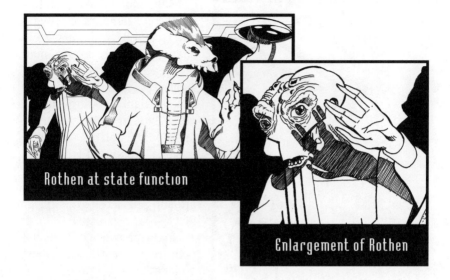

Rothen at state function

Enlargement of Rothen

Is their present appearance part of a deliberate attempt to look more appealing to human beings? Certainly their attractive appearance and soothing voices are effective at winning over some members of our culture. Rothen "missionaries" have been spotted many times on Earth and Terragen colonies, always skirting the fringes of visa and immigration laws, preaching to followers of Danek or "danekinite" fringe groups. Their essential message: that Rothen are the "long-lost patrons" of humankind.

They claim that they arrived on Earth 4.2 million years ago and began the Uplift process on early ancestors of Homo sapiens, but eventually left for ill-described reasons. Now, however, in our time of crisis, they have purportedly returned to finish the job of guiding us toward a vague but profound destiny. Even their reputation as mysterious and somewhat devious entities can seem to play in favor of this story, since these are just the traits one might expect from secret patrons, responsible for our "wolfling" race.

Could it be true? At present, a preponderance of opinion among Terragen, Kanten, and Tymbrimi scholars is swinging back to the notion that humans are that rarest phenomenon, True Wolflings, who achieved sapience completely on their own. In other words, we never had secret patrons at all. Various claimants to that role—including Rothen—are probably opportunists, fishing for followers among Earth's most gullible and distressed.

Rothen colony world

Still, the question of human Uplift remains unproved, and scientific opinions have changed before, so we must take each claim seriously. In support of the Rothen, their skill at data sabotage might help explain a great mystery—why Earth remained miscatalogued and ignored in Galactic records for so very long. Library Institute officials are still puzzled by this queer fact.

In the presence of potential converts, Rothen seem earnest and caring—like proud, endlessly patient parents of precocious children who still have a long way to go in order to achieve a grand destiny. But if a Rothen realizes that he is talking to a skeptic, or a Terragen official, he will exit the scene in great haste, vanishing with uncanny thoroughness and speed. Agents have already been assigned to this matter, but if you notice a Rothen activity cell at work, investigate and report.

Serentini

(ser-en-TEEN-ee) a Serentini /-ab Clauthin -ab Rihwlr -ab Mitahs /-ul Minatis -ul Sprwo

Proto-Serentini were a scuttling race, burrowing underground rock-cities to avoid the 300-mile-an-hour wind gusts of their home-world. They retain a hard, chitinous shell from that era, though their knack for spinning super-strong anchor cables reminds one more of

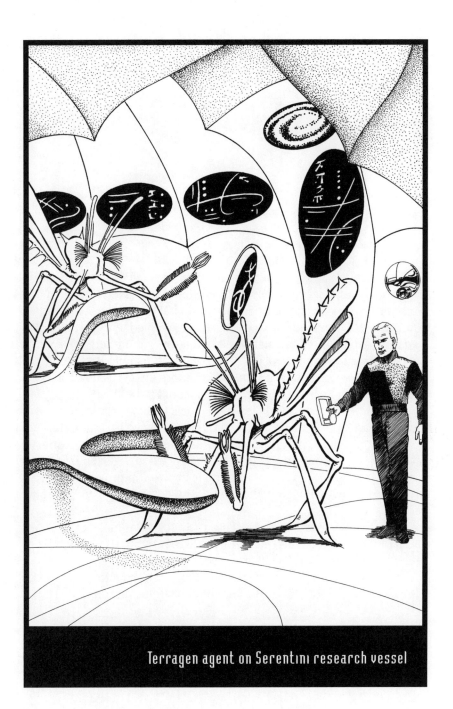

Terragen agent on Serentini research vessel

an Earthling spider. Serentini have reputations as diligent and punctilious without being fanatical. When mediators are needed, many call the Serentini. They seem to be withholding judgment on our "wolfling" race, giving us a chance to prove ourselves.

Seven Spin Clans

(seven spin clans) a Seven Spin Clans

The Seven Spin Clans are machine creatures left from the AI (artificial intelligence) wars of 280 million years ago (see "Revolt of the Data" in Timeline section). Unlike many digital races, they have official status in the Civilization of Five Galaxies, having gone to great lengths to assuage the almost instinctive fears that oxygen-breathing sapients feel toward autonomous robots. The Foresight Institute inspects regularly to make sure that both hardware and software follow rigorous procedures, to prevent unbridled reproduction.

There are hundreds of makes and models within the clan, and thousands of variations. Indeed, the Spin Clans mainly consist of solitary individuals that constantly redesign themselves, hiring out for complex tasks in widely dispersed locales. On rare occasion, a dozen or so clan members will gather to work on a single short-term project. They also prove useful working with the Zang and other hydrogen-breathing races.

Though they have been socially ostracized by most of the Oxy races of the Five Galaxies, Earth would like to establish diplomatic relations with this clan. If you meet sophisticated machine minds out there, express our interest. Promise nothing. Ask them to come by our embassy at Horst for a visit. But remind them to be discreet.

Negotiating trade with members of the Seven Spin Clans

Skiano

(sky-AN-o) a Skiano /-ul Hipnek -ul Kennn

Proto-Skiano were found 34 million years ago as semiaquatic nomads, migrating from tidal pool to tidal pool. They had gathered into informal trading groups, collectively bargaining among each other using hand signs and a crude type of blink-signaling with their upper set of eyes.

BIOLOGY ○ PSYCHOLOGY

Skiano are generally 2 to 2.5 meters tall, bipedal, with four eyes situated bird-like on the sides of a head shaped like the prow of a ship. Breathing is through blowholes in the top of the head, a trait left over from an amphibian past. Hands have long, suction-tipped fingers, once used in gathering anemone-like food from coral-like reefs. Their legs are bird-like, with webbed toes.

All of the four eyes have the ability to "flash," as part of the Skiano speech process. At first we suspected this was similar to Pring bioelectric lasers, but it is more like a firefly's glow. A nictitating membrane blinks over the Skiano's eye, making it flash. Most Skiano thoughtfully carry vodors to converse with non-Skiano.

The deal is everything in a Skiano mind. Even relationships between sexes are weighed on a quid-pro-quo basis. Adolescent Skiano negotiate with parents and peers for nearly all their needs. Philanthropy and charity are well-known social concepts, but only insofar as individuals can rationalize making a "deal" for a successful society for their descendants to live in.

And yet, Skiano have also been observed expressing great interest and curiosity about religion—whether exploring ancient tenets about the Progenitors, or delving into Judeo-Christian or Buddhist writings from Earth. Individual Skiano apparently seek ways to strike a bargain with the cosmos itself—as if performing the right rituals, or believing the right things, might buy ultimate success.

SOCIETY ○ CONTACT WITH EARTHLINGS

Skiano have embraced trading to a degree that "government" is a foreign concept. Instead they are bound by networks of contractually based mutual obligation, similar to libertarian fantasy-prescriptions from pre-contact Earth.

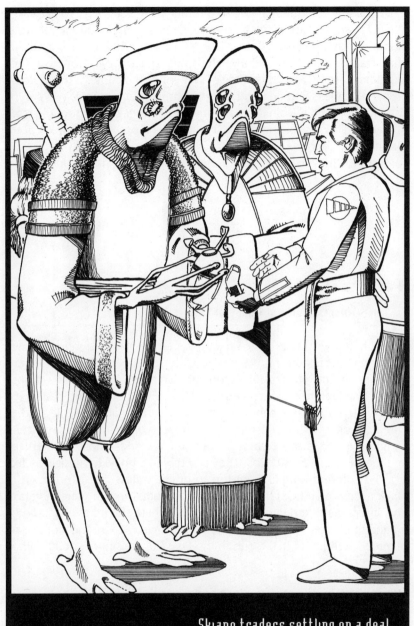

Skiano traders settling on a deal

If you are potentially going to interact with Skiano, try to acquire a Skiano-based vodor from a neutral source. As skilled negotiators, Skiano rarely make bad deals. They have a reputation for bargaining fairly, valuing long-term relationships over quick profit. However, they won't hesitate to take advantage of someone who came to the table ill-prepared. Unless you demand a signed privacy agreement, you can be sure they will sell information about your dealings throughout the trading lanes. This also means that Skiano can be excellent sources of information... for a fee.

Just be sure you count your fingers after shaking hands on a deal.

Tarseuh

(tar-SOO) a Tarseuh /-ul Thippt -ul Tchoost -ul Taxt

2.8 billion years ago, the Tarseuh were one of the mightiest known starfaring species during the post-Progenitor epoch. They led dozens of races in the successful campaign to resist the "Lions"—whose greedy wastage nearly wrecked Galactic civilization. Shortly after, the Tarseuh led six other senior races away, propagating the legend of "Great Ghosts," who will return whenever younger races face great danger. Beaked, armored bipeds, Tarseuh towered almost 3 meters tall and massed over 1,250 kilos. They resembled dignified, rhinoceros-like lizards. Coloring ranged from tan to bright yellow, all with brown or black accents. The Galactic Library notes that Tarseuh were vegetarians, living under a democratic oligarchy, where the masses appointed a handful of representatives to manage the clan. There has not been a recorded sighting of a Tarseuh in the Five Galaxies in over 600 million years.

Tarseuh portrait

Urs

(ERS) a Urs /-ab some /-ul a few

Urs are a centaur-like species with four legs and four small arm-like appendages. Two pouches, on each side of the female's forebody, contain one or two miniature husband-males, but at least one male is expelled when offspring are deposited for brooding. Three eyes form a triangle atop a snout at the end of a very flexible neck. The topmost eye is a lidless composite, sensitive to motion only, its purpose apparently to track the environs even when an Urs sleeps. Urs are obligate carnivores, though they accept cultured or synthetic flesh, if raw.

Free water is unusual on the original Urrish homeworld, Urchaka, where most moisture is held in the roots and stems of dense organic mats covering much of the planetary surface. This miracle saved the Mars-like world, but it also meant that animals derived all their water already bound in organic material. As a result, modern Urs are physiologically hydrophobic—they find liquid water unpleasantly caustic. Modern Urs will ingest it only under dire stress. Perhaps this way of life contributes to their short life span, averaging only thirty Earth years. Urs tend to seem in a hurry to accomplish as much as possible.

Tiny Urrish males barely qualify as sapient. Females are the leaders, warriors, and deal with outsiders. Their reproduction method implies a high natural birthrate, meaning they must constantly battle instinct in a Galactic milieu, where population control is seen as sacred duty. There are signs that this creates some tension.

Urs are a race of moderate power and wealth, active traders and voyagers, frequently encountered in port. They are decidedly nonhostile toward Clan Terragen. On an individual level, Earthlings and Urs often get along well, especially when sharing some interest, such as unconventional engineering. Urs show a curiosity about "wolfling" technologies—those we developed independently from Galactic traditions. For example, they actually like to help build and launch rockets, which other Galactics consider absurd.

SPECIAL NOTE: Do take care with liquid beverages near Urs, due to their distaste for freestanding water. Humans should also exercise careful hygiene around them, because Urs find our body odor rather unpleasant. Human travelers report having similar reactions to Urrish aroma. Urs-specific nasal scent-killers are available from Supply Division.

The smell thing is unfortunate. Otherwise, they seem a likeable folk. Just don't waste their time. They have little of it, and want to get things done.

Z'Tang

(z-*click*-TANG) a Z'Tang /-ab Kl'Brouge' -ab Jerbtk /-ul Z'boal -ul Z'ruq

Like their patrons, the Kl'Brouge', the Z'Tang seem to crave a Galactic position equivalent to the old-Swiss on Earth, having spent several million years being completely neutral in Galactic affairs, neither angering nor tempting any major clans. Their second reputation is for excellence at hyperspatial and T-Point navigation. Z'Tang threadriders are among the best, though lately Dolphins have been giving them a run for their money.

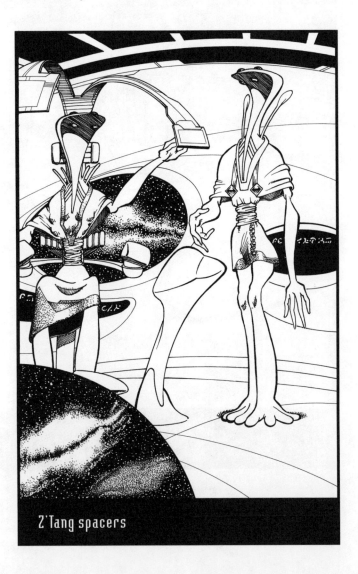

Z'Tang spacers

A final Note to All Agents

Once again, your attention must turn to security—this guide is a top-secret document. Our experts believe most aliens will be puzzled and unable to make sense of a "wolfling-style" book with paper pages. But we cannot count on that. If you have reason to believe this volume has been snooped or copied without permission, notify your instructors immediately!

Of course, you will cover much of the same material—in far greater detail—in your regular courses, such as Galactography, Non-Terran BioPsych, Diplomatic Ritual, Earthclan Security, Catastrophe Prevention, and Understanding Basic Transindowetbs of the Five Galaxies. To quick-scan further information, or to try out your abilities in some *realistic contact scenarios,* set your neuralseeker to

***** or ******.

Or else try out contact scenarios at the following:

http://www.lenaghalienfactory.com/

http://www.sjgames.com/uplift/

http://www.davidbrin.com/

(For now, at least, extraterrestrials seem to find the Old Web almost as unfathomable as paper books! One reason we still keep the creaky old thing around.)

If you are a neo-Dolphin agent, you can gain further insights by swimming far offshore and adjusting your listening modes to a sub-oceanic contemplation resonance named "Deep Blue Dream of High Perilous Maybes." A wise Humpback Whale will be available to guide your queries—most weekdays around noon, Zulu time.

Go forth and help us survive.

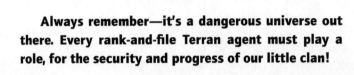

Always remember—it's a dangerous universe out there. Every rank-and-file Terran agent must play a role, for the security and progress of our little clan!

Acknowledgments

We cast our thoughts backward, in fond memory, to some heroes of the long-ago 20th and 21st centuries whose efforts helped make the world of Terragen Agents possible. These revered ancients include Steve Jackson, Cheryl Brigham, Mark Grygier, Alberto Monteiro, Trent Shipley, William Stoddard, Bill Haines, Ruben Krasnopolsky, and of course the legendary Stefan Jones, whose grasp of this universe is second to none, especially his testimony about Pring and Norruhk! And Sandra Lenagh, who started the whole process of communication with promising Terran agents.

Without them, the world you see before you at this moment would not have been the same.

Kevin Lenagh & David Brin
Supervisors of Illicit Wolfling Training Texts

Clan Index

CLAN SORO
(page 31)

Luber
　Puber
　　Hul
　　　Soro
　　　　Kisa
　　　　　Pila
　　　　　　Pring
　　　　Gello
　　　　Bahtwin
　　　　Forski

CLAN SYNTHIAN
(page 52)

Pee'oot
　Chelbi
　　Tharner
　　Synthian
　　　Wazoon

CLAN THENNANIN
(page 60)

Tothtoon
　Rosh
　　Kosh
　　　Wortl
　　　　Thennanin
　　　　　Paimin
　　　　　Rammin
　　　　　Ynnin
　　　　　Olumimun
　　　　　Garthling

CLAN FONNIR
(page 76)

Fonnir
　Norruhk

Learn the Secrets of Uplift!

*The Five Galaxies are a tough neighborhood...
and mankind is the new kid on the block.*

Of the thousands of races in a galaxy full of aliens, ours is the only starfaring species that claims to have evolved on its own, without having been genetically engineered, or "uplifted," by a patron species. Along with our own new clients – modified dolphins and chimpanzees – humanity faces a jealous universe. The ancient senior patron clans can't decide whether to enslave the upstart races of Terra or just wipe them out.

Those stodgy Galactics have wealth, power, and incredible technology. The dolphins, chimps, and humans of Earthclan have guts, originality, and a handful of allies . . . and they won't give up.

Now there's an official roleplaying sourcebook for David Brin's cosmically popular Uplift universe. **GURPS Uplift** has full descriptions of many important worlds and alien races, making it the perfect complement to **Contacting Aliens: The Illustrated Guide To David Brin's Uplift Universe.**

GURPS Uplift also gives you detailed background on the many ways that Terragens agents fight for the freedom of Earthclan, while seeking to uncover secrets older than the stars themselves! It also includes complete rules for creating – and Uplifting – new species. This is the best alien-generating system yet devised for designing your own believable alien worlds, races, cultures, and individuals . . . as friends of Earthclan or as foes!

This is a sourcebook for any roleplaying system, and is vital background for fans of the Uplift series.

Visit **www.sjgames.com/uplift/** for more about this book and for other Uplift source material.

"Nobody on Planet Earth knows the Uplift Universe better than Stefan Jones, or has a better instinct for how adventures can be spun off its many possibilities. GURPS Uplift is a marvel, offering game options that are almost limitless."
  —David Brin, author of **Startide Rising** and **The Uplift War**